Damn, she was in trouble.

Lying in the dark with him, side by side in separate beds, while their child slept nearby, her desire intensified, becoming so strong she couldn't sleep. Her entire body burned with need.

In the bed next to her, Tucker's ragged breathing told her that he had the same problem. "Tucker?" she said, then mentally kicked herself for speaking. "Are you…?"

"Yes, I'm thinking about you," he said, his voice harsh. "Fantasizing about you. And yes, Lucy, I want you. More than you could ever believe."

She gasped as need and desire blossomed through her. So much for careful resolutions and planning. She could no more resist this man than she could stop breathing.

If that made her a fool, then so be it.

* * *

"Like" us on Facebook at
www.facebook.com/RomanticSuspenseBooks
and check us out on www.Harlequin.com!

Dear Reader,

As often is the case with writers, *The CEO's Secret Baby* stemmed from my thinking "what if?" What if a man had been held prisoner for a year and when set free, returned home to find that he might as well have become a ghost? Believing him dead, his girlfriend had gone on without him, forging a new relationship with his best friend. Even more shockingly, she'd been pregnant and he has a three-month-old son!

And then I had to wonder what it would be like to be her, having lost the man you loved, carried and birthed his baby and, after a year, forged a tentative alliance with his best friend. Only to have all this blow up in her face when her first love shows up, not dead after all. Throw in a Mexican drug cartel and ten million missing dollars, and things start to heat up even more.

A fascinating concept, yes? I hope I've done it justice. For this book, we return to my beloved Boulder, Colorado, in the summer, normally a carefree time, but not for them. I hope you enjoy reading this book as much as I enjoyed writing it.

Karen Whiddon

KAREN WHIDDON

The CEO's Secret Baby

ROMANTIC
SUSPENSE

If you purchased this book without a cover you should be aware
that this book is stolen property. It was reported as "unsold and
destroyed" to the publisher, and neither the author nor the
publisher has received any payment for this "stripped book."

Recycling programs
for this product may
not exist in your area.

ISBN-13: 978-0-373-27732-2

THE CEO'S SECRET BABY

Copyright © 2011 by Karen Whiddon

All rights reserved. Except for use in any review, the reproduction
or utilization of this work in whole or in part in any form by any
electronic, mechanical or other means, now known or hereafter
invented, including xerography, photocopying and recording, or in
any information storage or retrieval system, is forbidden without
the written permission of the publisher, Harlequin Enterprises Limited,
225 Duncan Mill Road, Don Mills, Ontario M3B 3K9, Canada.

This is a work of fiction. Names, characters, places and incidents are
either the product of the author's imagination or are used fictitiously, and
any resemblance to actual persons, living or dead, business establishments,
events or locales is entirely coincidental.

This edition published by arrangement with Harlequin Books S.A.

For questions and comments about the quality of this book
please contact us at Customer_eCare@Harlequin.ca.

® and TM are trademarks of Harlequin Books S.A., used under license.
Trademarks indicated with ® are registered in the United States Patent
and Trademark Office, the Canadian Trade Marks Office and in other
countries.

www.Harlequin.com

Printed in U.S.A.

Books by Karen Whiddon

Romantic Suspense

★*One Eye Open* #1301
★*One Eye Closed* #1365
★*Secrets of the Wolf* #1397
The Princess's Secret Scandal #1416
Bulletproof Marriage #1484
★★*Black Sheep P.I.* #1513
★★*The Perfect Soldier* #1557
★★*Profile for Seduction* #1629
Colton's Christmas Baby #1636
The CEO's Secret Baby #1662

★*The Pack*
★★*The Cordasic Legacy*

Nocturne

★*Cry of the Wolf* #7
★*Touch of the Wolf* #12
★*Dance of the Wolf* #45
★*Wild Wolf* #67
★*Lone Wolf* #103

Signature Collections

Beyond the Dark
  "Soul of the Wolf"

KAREN WHIDDON

started weaving fanciful tales for her younger brothers at the age of eleven. Amidst the Catskill Mountains of New York, then the Rocky Mountains of Colorado, she fueled her imagination with the natural beauty of the rugged peaks and spun stories of love that captivated her family's attention.

Karen now lives in north Texas, where she shares her life with her very own hero of a husband and three doting dogs. Also an entrepreneur, she divides her time between the business she started and writing the contemporary romantic suspense and paranormal romances that readers enjoy. You can email Karen at KWhiddon1@aol.com or write to her at P.O. Box 820807, Fort Worth, TX 76182. Fans of her writing can also check out her website, www.karenwhiddon.com.

To my husband's family,
who have also become mine. Floyd, Sarah,
and Lavenia. Know that I love you dearly.

Chapter 1

The Fourth of July began like any other summer morning. Lucy Knowlton woke up, well-rested after a dreamless night, and showered. Then, with sunlight streaming lemon yellow through her open kitchen window, she ate her normal breakfast—multigrain Cheerios with sliced strawberries and almond milk.

The early morning air was still cool, though she knew the temperature would continue to rise. All in all, she felt…good. Surprisingly upbeat. Maybe because she'd actually slept well. She supposed she should feel grateful that she'd finally stopped having nightmares about Tucker and how he must have felt when the plane went down.

Rinsing her dishes in the sink and stacking them in the dishwasher, she'd just finished when her three-month-old baby, Eli, cried to let her know he was awake and wanted to be fed. The obvious delight in his bright blue eyes as he latched on to her breast made her happy and she smiled. Vaguely amazed at the soft happiness she felt, she thought her smiles came a little bit more frequently these days. Or at least she hoped so.

After all, she had so much to be thankful for. Though Tucker's absence had left her with a gaping hole in her life, over time she'd tried to pull the tattered edges closer together. A week, a month, a day, a minute at a time.

Still, at any given moment she could calculate exactly how long it had been since Tucker had died. Today marked one year, two weeks and one day. Ignoring the ever-present ache of missing him, she spent the rest of the morning puttering around the house doing myriad daily chores.

Humming nursery rhymes to entertain Eli in his playpen, she washed two loads of laundry, cleaned her bathroom and mopped the kitchen floor. In between she changed Eli's diaper, sang to him, rocked him and cuddled him. She found if she kept busy, she didn't think so much. All in all, life kept getting better.

Come early afternoon, she put Eli down for a nap. At three months old, he slept a lot still, for which she was guiltily grateful, as she couldn't seem to find enough hours in the day to get everything done.

Especially today. Glad her energy was high, because she still had a lot to do before the holiday celebration later. And it was very important to her that she attend the fireworks display, even though she wouldn't take the baby inside the stadium because of the noise. She'd watch from a distance and try to stay until the very end. She planned to do this in honor of Tucker—the Fourth of July had been his favorite holiday. Last year, she'd been too devastated to even consider attending any kind of celebration.

This year, she'd do it up right.

So, on this day of all days, she pushed aside her grief at his untimely death and tried to feel lighthearted. At least she could count on Sean Morey, Tucker's best friend and her brand-new fiancé, to help her as they watched the fireworks display explode in vibrant colors in the velvet sky above them.

When the doorbell rang, the muted sound of the clear, mellow chimes made her smile again. A gift from Sean, he'd installed them only a few days ago. She loved the way they sounded, too quiet to wake Eli, but loud enough to let her know someone was at the door. Her obvious delight in the chimes had to be the reason why Sean rang them now instead of just walking inside as he usually did.

Keeping her smile firmly in place so Sean wouldn't worry because she always looked so sad, she hurried to the front door and pulled it open.

"Hey, you!" As she took in the sight of the tall, broad-shouldered man standing on her front step, her less than genuine smile froze in place.

A ghost looked back at her from sapphire blue eyes exactly like her son's. Her heart skipped a beat and she struggled to breathe. Not Sean, as she'd supposed. But Tucker, instead. Tucker Drover, the man who, for all intents and purposes, had died a little over one year ago in a fiery plane crash in Mexico.

Died. She'd attended his funeral, wept over his grave.

This. Could. Not. Be. Real.

Had she finally lost it? Closing her eyes, she inhaled and counted to three before opening them again.

He was still there, his shadow long and dark behind him in the bright sunlight. Standing on her doorstep, staring back at her, his amazing eyes roaming over her as intimate as a touch, making her shiver.

Tucker? Really? She couldn't speak, unable to trust her eyes. He continued to watch at her, his expectant smile fading as she continued to stare in shocked disbelief.

"Say something," he entreated. "Welcome me home, curse me out, I don't know. But say *something,* Lucy. Do something."

Though he sounded weary, his tone low and ragged, she would have recognized that beloved voice anywhere. Tucker. Tucker was…alive? How could this be?

Paralyzed, she tried to form words to demand answers. Pain warred with hope, agony with desire. Tucker was dead. He couldn't be standing here on her doorstep. Was this a trick? Some kind of hallucination? One of those nightmares that she'd thought she'd vanquished?

Had she finally completely gone insane?

"Lucy?" he rasped, narrowing his eyes. "Are you all right?"

She didn't faint, even though the edges of her vision momentarily went gray and the ground seemed to tilt in front of her. Staring at him, she tried to remember to breathe, still dimly certain that this couldn't be real.

"Lucy?" he said again, cocking his head and studying her with that serious, glinting blue gaze she'd always loved. Finally, hope slammed into her, mingling with joy and shock and disbelief and…love.

"Tucker," she managed, her throat closing up as words failed her. But it didn't matter; nothing did, because Tucker was here, with her. Alive. He'd come back alive.

She let her gaze devour him, feeling starved. Taking in his rugged, beloved face, his broad shoulders and muscular arms suddenly wasn't enough. She needed to *feel* him, his arms around her. She needed to bury her face in the crook of his neck, to inhale the woodsy scent of him. She needed reassurance that she wasn't dreaming, that indeed, this was real.

"Is it…?" Her voice came out in a croak. Trying to understand, to assimilate how he could both be here and not, she took a step forward, dizzy, swaying, confused. "Tucker? It's you? It's really you?"

Head tilted quizzically, he gave the smallest of nods. Still, he made no move to take her in his arms, to hold her close. She didn't understand why not, didn't really care at this point. Tucker was home!

She made the first move herself. Taking a step forward, she threw herself at him, joy filling her. Her heart beat a frantic tattoo in her chest as she wrapped her arms around him, holding on like she never wanted to let him go. Which she didn't. Not ever.

Gradually, she became conscious of the fact that, though he hugged her back, something was…different. He held himself stiffly. Rather than relaxing into her embrace, he seemed to be only going through the motions.

She pulled back and looked up at him. While his eyes were still the same shocking shade of sapphire, the look in them was not. Anger and bitterness, rather than love, warred in his amazing eyes.

Anger? At her?

As she eyed him, Tucker, this man who'd disappeared from her life so suddenly and violently, whose supposed death had ripped the heart from her chest and stripped all the joy from her world, she suddenly realized she was angry, too. Furious.

Glaring up at him, she stepped back, keeping hold

of his arms. "What happened to you? Where have you been all this time? Why didn't you call?"

"I couldn't," he said simply. "After they got me out, they wouldn't let me have access to a phone, even after my debriefing. Take my word for it. If I could have called, I would have."

"They? Debriefing?" She needed answers. She deserved answers. "Tucker?" she kept her voice level. "I don't understand. What do you mean?"

"Sorry." Letting out a breath, he dragged his hand across his chin. "It's a long story and I'm dead on my feet. Can I come in?"

Without hesitation, she stepped aside, gesturing for him to move past her. Once he did, she closed the door, quietly clicking the lock into place. All of her motions were slow and deliberate, as though the simple routine of performing regular gestures could make everything normal again.

Normal. As if. For a heartbeat, one frozen moment, she let her own anger simmer, then took a deep breath and ruthlessly pushed it back down inside her, allowing the joy to come flooding back. Tucker was alive. He'd returned home; miraculously back from the dead, like Lazarus pushing aside his funeral shroud. Alive.

They would rejoice, they should rejoice, but first, surely he owed her a few words of explanation. He'd disappeared for over a year, made no effort to contact her, and let her believe he was dead. She needed to understand why.

Trembling from the effort of remaining calm, she turned again to face him. He watched her, expression impassive, detached when he should have been joyful. This, she also didn't understand.

"You seem surprised to see me," he commented, one

corner of his mouth lifting in a twisted sort of smile. "It's been a while, hasn't it, Lucy girl?"

Despite herself, warmth curled inside of her at the familiar nickname. She hadn't been called that since the last time she'd seen him.

"Of course I'm surprised." Her voice came out wobbly. Taking a deep breath, she eyed him, full of a cautious sort of love—and pain. "Seriously, I really need to know where you've been all this time. We thought you were dead."

"Dead?" He lifted a brow, inadvertently making her insides clench from the sheer masculine beauty of his rugged features. "Really?"

Scarcely able to believe that he wasn't taking her seriously, she nodded. "Yes. We were officially notified that you were dead."

"We?"

"Sean and I. Remember him? Your best friend? Or did you forget about him, too?" Guilt and anger propelling her, she swept by him, leading the way into her living room, hyper-conscious of him right behind. Alive. Alive.

"We thought you were dead," she repeated. "I wept over your picture at your funeral—we didn't even have a body to bury. Your parents flew in from Nepal." Her eyes filled with tears and she turned away to hide it.

Gathering her composure, she continued. "I've mourned you, Tucker. You don't know how much I've grieved over you. And now…you're here. Alive and waltzing into the house as though nothing has happened, asking me if I'm surprised to see you."

Perching on the edge of the couch, she gestured for him to take a seat in the overstuffed chair he'd always claimed as his own. "I don't understand. Explain this to me. I don't even know what page you're on."

"I'm sorry," he said softly, sounding both bewildered and sad. "I've been through so much. I'm confused and recovering. But I swear to you, no one told me you thought I died."

He took a deep breath and blew it back out again. "I was in pretty bad shape. The ones who rescued me, they were mostly concerned with making sure I didn't really die to tell me anything."

Again with the odd, sketchy references.

"Once they got me back to health, they had questions of their own that they wanted answered," he continued. "Too many of them to remember. And yes, I've been told I was gone over a year, though time passes differently when you're in that sort of situation. In this, I had no choice in the matter."

"I still don't understand. I guess you think what you're saying is clear, but it makes no sense to me."

Slowly, he nodded. "I'm sorry. Let me start over."

Crossing her arms to keep from touching him, she caught her breath as she belatedly realized exhaustion showed white around the edge of his mouth. Despite his tanned skin and corded, muscular arms, he was thin as a rail, too, though his shoulders were still as broad.

And he was just as beautiful.

"Start at the beginning," she offered.

"Okay. Let me tell you as much as I remember," he said. "One minute I was striding through the Mexican fields with the man I went to meet. You remember. His name was Carlos, and he claimed to have grown a completely new and fantastic strain of coffee beans."

He'd gone to obtain samples to see if his company,

Boulder's Best Brew, would be interested in distributing them.

"I felt a blow at the back of my head like an explosion," he continued. "After that, I regained consciousness chained and was trussed like an animal, with a headache the size of Denver."

His eyes were haunted as he paused. "I had no idea where I was. I'd gone down in the wilds of the Mexican jungle. Carlos, the two employees who'd traveled with me, as well as my Spanish interpreter, had vanished— either dead or captured, too. I was a prisoner, with no way to contact you or Sean or even the American embassy. Worse, I had no idea why."

Though he paused as if inviting comments, Lucy didn't interrupt. Holding her gaze, he swallowed and continued.

"They tortured me enough to put me on the tattered edge of crazy. Without my interpreters, I couldn't understand most of what they asked me, though after a while I realized they thought I'd stolen something. Instead, I tried to figure out a way out of there, a way home to you. I began making up lies to keep them from torturing me more. But no matter what they did to me, I couldn't tell them what they wanted because I truly didn't know."

"They? Who were they?" she asked, her throat aching at the haunting look on his face. "Who did this to you?"

He winced as he shrugged. "As best as I could tell, I was held prisoner by a major Mexican drug cartel."

"Did you tell them that they had the wrong person?"

"I tried. But since my Spanish is extremely limited, the explanation I tried to give them fell on deaf ears."

"You're lucky they didn't kill you."

"I don't know about that," he said. "At first, I dreamed of escape, of home. After a while, I mostly dreamt of death. I wanted them to just go ahead and kill me. Get it over with. But they wouldn't end my suffering and let me die."

His voice broke and he looked down briefly before continuing. "I still don't understand why not. Drug cartels like this one are ruthless. They usually kill spies or anyone who pissed them off without blinking. You've heard the stories of the mass graves found near the border, where they lined their enemies up near a shallow ditch and shot them in the back. But not me." He sounded bitter, but this time, she understood why.

"For whatever reason, they kept me alive, using me as entertainment. Bored? Go torture the prisoner. Can't sleep? Then make sure the prisoner doesn't, either."

She shuddered at his words, aching, wanting both to stop him and let him go on, hoping maybe once he'd told the story he could purge the horror from his system.

"I hated them with a passion," he continued. "Though I was careful not to reveal the depths of my rage. As it became more and more clear that they had no intention of killing me, I knew I had to get out. If I could escape, I could try to get home.

"I tried to formulate a plan, but came up with nothing. The only thing I knew for sure was escaping wouldn't be easy. My captors fed me just enough to keep me breathing, no more. Weakened by starvation, I could barely walk, never mind hike through miles of jungle to search out civilization and rescue."

"Oh, Tucker. I'm so sorry."

He went on talking as though he hadn't heard her. "Basically, unless there was a miracle, I knew I was a dead man. I'd been in the wrong place at the wrong time. My luck had finally run out."

"How'd you escape?" she asked.

His gaze cleared and he dipped his chin. "A rival drug faction ambushed my captors. The ensuing shootout left several dead, many more wounded, while the rest fled. I was left, alone and forgotten in my jail cell. By then, circumstances had extinguished even the smallest flicker of hope. I simply waited to die of starvation and neglect. I hoped I wouldn't linger—after all, how long could my body hang on by the proverbial thread?"

He went silent.

"But you were rescued. By whom?" she prompted.

"The DEA had someone undercover. Apparently, they learned of my capture and got me out. After that, everything was a blur. The next thing I knew, I found myself in a hospital in San Antonio, Texas, under heavy guard. I was questioned by some military-looking types, who'd claimed to be DEA. My repeated attempts to contact my family had been met with refusal. I was told only that making any outside contact could endanger my life. I was so heavily guarded that I felt like I was a prisoner again."

"But they finally let you go?" she asked. "Do you have any idea why?"

"No. But once my fever was gone and I could keep solid food down and stand unassisted, they finally released me. They even arranged for transport, driving me here in one of those nondescript, law-enforcement type vehicles and dropping me off." He flashed her a smile, a shadow of the carefree grins she remembered. "And here I am."

"And here you are," Lucy echoed. She wanted to go to him and hold him, but instead she kept herself still, hands clenched together. Her anger now directed at herself, she wondered how to tell him what she'd done. Tucker had already been through hell.

Before he'd disappeared and supposedly died, she'd waited forever for him to propose to her. Instead, he'd let his wanderlust haul him all over the globe, unwilling or unable to commit.

And now, believing him dead for over a year, she'd gone and gotten herself engaged to his best friend.

She felt ill, positively sick. Barely two weeks ago she'd agreed to become Sean's wife.

"Why did they think you were dead?" she cried. "I would have moved heaven and earth to find you if I'd had the tiniest bit of hope that you'd survived. But they said you didn't. They said it was you."

"I…" Closing his eyes as though by doing so, he could block out all emotion, he shook his shaggy head. "I don't know. They didn't say anything about this when they debriefed me. You really thought I was…"

"Yes. Dead." She spoke deliberately. "You were killed in the plane crash."

"Lucy, listen to me. I wasn't in a plane crash," he said, his raspy voice simmering with undercurrents of lingering fury mixed with exhaustion.

So they were both angry. And maybe one of them was crazy. But which one? She was beginning to wonder.

"There was a plane crash," she insisted. "We were told you were dead. The plane went down, exploded on impact, killing all on board. They identified Bruno, and Carlos, the man you'd gone to meet. And they found your wallet, though the…remains were too badly charred and scattered to know for sure."

"Who told you this?"

"The authorities, of course."

"Oh, Lucy."

Unable to sit still any longer, she got up and crossed the room to stand in front of him. "I thought you were dead." Unthinking, she reached out her hand to him.

While he didn't recoil, not exactly, he shifted and moved enough so that her outstretched fingers didn't come in contact with him at all.

As she slowly lowered her arm, he stared at her silently, as a stranger might, offering no embrace, no kiss, nothing to show that they'd loved each other once.

Twisting the ring on her finger, she realized it was a very good thing she and Sean had gotten engaged.

Tucker's gaze followed the motion. "Let me see your hand."

The ring. Sean's ring. Slowly, she lifted her hand, wincing as he took it, raising it so the large ring glittered in the sunlight streaming through her front window.

"Nice." Jaw clenched, he fairly spat the word. "Who?"

"I thought you were dead," she cried.

"Who?" he demanded again.

Taking a deep breath, she told him. "Sean."

He jerked back, clearly stunned. "Sean? Sean Morey?"

"Yes." She inhaled, exhaled, scrambling for a rational explanation and finding none, except…there was always the truth. "I waited for you, but—"

"Obviously," he bit out. "Whatever happened to I'll love you forever?"

"Don't be like that." She threw her words at him, using anger to cover her pain. "You were dead, Tucker. For over a year, I mourned you. Sean was here for me. Even…"

"Even before my so-called death?"

Inwardly she flinched, but reminding herself that she'd resolved to stick with the truth, she lifted her chin. "Sean and I were friends, Tucker. Nothing more. You know that."

"Obviously you were more than that."

Ignoring his sarcastic reply, she kept on as if he hadn't spoken. "Friends," she said firmly. "But while you were traveling around the globe in your never-ending search for the elusive perfect coffee bean, Sean stayed here and kept me company."

"I'll bet he did." More than bitter, he sounded furious. As if he had a right to be.

"I waited for you," she sighed. "And if you hadn't died, I'd probably still be waiting for you to get tired of roaming the world." This was an old argument and one that had never made the slightest impression on him before.

Nor did it appear to now. Eyes narrowed, he continued to watch her. "So you're telling me that less than one year after my so-called death, you got engaged to my best friend?"

Squaring her shoulders, she stared right back. "You were gone an entire year. Twelve long months without a single word from you."

"It. Was. Not. My. Fault." He ground out the words.

She almost hung her head. Instead, she lifted her chin and let him see the agony in her eyes. "Nor was it mine."

"Let me see if I've got this straight," he said. "I died and came back to life, and returned home to find out you've moved on."

"I just did the best I could to try and live my life." The ache in her throat told her she was perilously close to tears. Circumstances and events had changed them both. Things could never be the same between them.

Except, she thought, horrified. There had been another change, the biggest one of all. Now, she had a son. *They* had a son. Eli, Tucker's child. Even though she'd only learned of her pregnancy after the plane crash, even if things had been different and Tucker had returned a year ago from his coffee expedition, she would have been unwilling to use their baby as a reason to tie him to her.

Just as she wouldn't use it now. Still, she had to tell him.

As she opened her mouth to speak, her front door opened, making her jump.

Sean. Ah, crap, she'd forgotten. Glancing once more at Tucker, she hurried over to the foyer. "Sean, there's—"

"Happy Fourth," Sean interrupted, pulling her close in a one-armed hug and kissing her hard on the mouth before releasing her. Closing the front door quietly behind him so he wouldn't wake the baby, he came inside, carrying several plastic grocery bags.

"Sean, I need—"

Oblivious, he pulled her in again for another quick kiss. "Hey," he said, grinning. "I snagged a perfect watermelon and picked up some of those diet drinks you love so much."

"Great. Um, there's been a change of plans." Wiping her hands nervously down the front of her shorts, she once again found herself struggling to find the right words. Sean eyed her curiously, his smile gradually fading.

Finally, she simply moved aside and gestured toward

the living room and the man who stood silently watching them.

Taking a step forward, Sean's expression changed when he caught sight of Tucker. Shock flashed across his face, then disbelief, and then finally, joy.

"Tucker?" Sean managed, talking a halting step forward. "Is it really you?"

"Yep," Tucker rasped, eyeing his former best friend with narrowed eyes. "It's me, all right."

"Tucker?" Juggling his bags, Sean moved closer. He glanced from Tucker to Lucy, then back again. "How... What?"

When Tucker didn't answer, Lucy swallowed and took over. "It's really him, Sean. He's—"

"Actually here," Tucker finished for her, pushing a hand wearily through his hair. "In the flesh, still alive, though barely." Swaying slightly, he flashed Sean a tight-lipped, humorless smile. "Surprised?"

"Surprised isn't the word!" Depositing the bags on the floor, Sean crossed the room and guy-hugged his best friend, grinning. If he noticed Tucker's lack of response, he didn't comment. Instead, he grimaced before stepping back and cocking his head. "Where the hell have you been, man? We thought you were dead."

"Long story," Tucker replied. When his gaze found Lucy's, she read a regretful warning in his blue eyes. Warning against what? Against Sean, his—no, their— best friend?

Damn. Stunned, Lucy continued to study him, unable to help herself. His auburn hair looked much the same, though duller. He wore it longer and much shaggier. His clothing hung on his tall frame and had the battered look of worn hand-me-downs. The sallow color of his skin spoke of illness. Still, she found him too beautiful for her own good.

She felt a moment of sorrow, which she squashed. Shaking her head, she swallowed, the knot in her chest tightening. Blinking back sudden and unwanted tears, she busied herself with grabbing the grocery bags up off the floor and carrying them to the kitchen so she could unpack them. Busy work, busy work, as if by keeping her hands occupied she could hold back the flood of emotions.

Still, she could only hide out in the kitchen for so long. Eventually, she had to go back to where the two men continued to talk quietly.

Returning, she got about halfway there when a loud wail split the air, making her freeze in her tracks. Eli, waking up from his nap. And she hadn't yet managed to tell Tucker that he had a son.

Chapter 2

Cripes.

Tucker stiffened, glancing from Lucy to Sean, then back to Lucy. "What was that?"

Opening her mouth to speak, Lucy decided she'd be better off showing rather than telling. "Just a minute," she said, and hurried from the room to get her son. *Their* son, actually.

Screwing his chubby little face up in preparation for a louder cry, Eli whimpered instead as he caught sight of her. His blue eyes, so like his father's, fixed on her face and he cooed happily. The sight of him made Lucy grin despite herself. She reached for him, lifting him and settling him so his head was on her shoulder. He smelled of baby powder and milk. Perfection, all in one small bundle.

"Hi, Eli," she murmured, patting his back softly. "Did you have a nice nap?"

"You have a son?" Behind her, Tucker's voice, completely devoid of emotion.

"Yes." She tensed up again, which alarmed Eli. His bright eyes went wide and he scrunched his face, as though trying to decide whether or not to cry. "Shhh, sweetheart." She gave him a soft kiss, before turning slowly.

Tucker stood in the doorway, frozen. The look on his face fell somewhere between shock and disbelief. At least, she thought sadly, it wasn't horror.

At least he hadn't died not knowing he had a son, as she'd thought.

From somewhere, she dredged up a smile, not sure why this miraculous homecoming wasn't going at all the way she'd always imagined it would, back when she'd refused to give up hope that they'd find Tucker alive.

"You and Sean have a son," he said, his voice wooden and bleak.

"No, not Sean and I. *We* have a son," she corrected. "You and I. Tucker, this is Eli, your boy. He's three months old as of last week." Taking a deep breath, she braced herself for his reaction. "Though I suspected before you left, I learned I truly was pregnant right after you left for Mexico. Right before you…died."

Clearly in shock, Tucker only stared, his chiseled features emotionless.

"The CEO's secret baby," Sean joked. Neither Lucy nor Tucker responded.

Oblivious to it all, Eli cooed again, turning his sweet little mouth into her neck, blindly searching for sustenance. Immediately, her breasts tingled as her milk came in. She'd have to let him nurse soon. But first, he needed to meet his father.

Still Tucker didn't move, standing frozen near the

entrance to the room, looking huge and awkward and completely out of place. Her heart melted a little bit more.

"It's okay," she said, reassuring both the man and the child. "Come meet him. He won't bite."

As Tucker stepped forward, she lowered their baby from her shoulder, holding him in the crook of her arm.

Still silent, Tucker shot her a questioning look before peering into his son's small, round face. Eli gurgled, wide-eyed and grinning. His bright blue eyes, reflected back in Tucker's, fixated for a moment on his father's craggy face. Then he wrinkled his mouth again, and she knew he was on the verge of screaming in that ear-piercing way babies have. He was hungry, after all.

A second later, he began to cry. Shifting him in her arms, she rocked him slowly, murmuring wordless endearments and crooning soothing sounds.

Immediately, Tucker took a step backward, his expression closed and unreadable again. But not before she saw the flash of pain.

"Hey E, it's all right." Sean appeared in the doorway behind Tucker. Eli broke off midcry at the sound of Sean's cheery voice. His chubby face smoothed out and he cooed, happy again. He really did like Sean. After all, until now Sean had been like a father figure to him. The only one he'd known in his short time on earth.

"Let me see him," Sean said, flashing an easy smile at Tucker before reaching to take Eli from Lucy.

As Sean took the baby and began rocking him, Tucker's expression shut down even further, becoming a frozen mask.

"He knows Sean, that's all," she said softly. "You've got to give him time to get to know you, too."

Tucker made a sound, a cross between a grunt and a curse, which could have meant anything. Exhaling, Lucy stifled the urge to comfort him. Clearly, he felt Sean had robbed him of not only her, but his family. A family he hadn't even known he had.

Oblivious to the undercurrent swirling in the room, or pretending to be, Sean looked from one to the other, smiling as he cradled the baby expertly in the crook of his arm. "I think we've all got some catching up to do," he said. "Eli's an amazing kid. You must be so proud. Welcome home, buddy."

Gaze still shuttered, Tucker nodded. "Thanks." He studied Eli for a moment more before his eyes found Lucy. The starkness of the pain she saw there felt like a knife twisting in her heart.

Her own gut twisted. True, she and Sean were engaged. But even before his so-called death, Tucker had been well aware she'd wanted the entire white picket fence and family thing. He'd told her right before he left for Mexico that he wasn't sure he could provide that. Now, more than a year later, he'd returned from the dead to learn another man had stepped up to the plate.

So she'd gotten engaged to his best friend. She had a child to think about now. At least Sean had been willing to provide for and, more important, love another man's baby.

She opened her mouth to say exactly that, but Tucker beat her to it.

"We need to talk," he said, his low voice simmering with anger and pain.

At the harsh tone, Eli whimpered and turned his face searchingly in her general direction before letting out a lusty cry, then another.

"He's hungry," she said, as her feeding-time breast-tingling intensified, making her pray she didn't leak. "I'd better nurse him."

Sean transferred the baby effortlessly to her. When she finished getting him settled, she turned her back to the two men and unfastened her blouse and nursing bra. As soon as Eli latched on to her nipple, she grabbed a baby blanket from the crib and covered herself and Eli. She turned back to face the two men, only to find Tucker watching, his expression shuttered.

Once again, she ached to go to him, pull him into an embrace like she used to, as she'd dreamed of doing for so many agonizing, painful nights after learning of his death—but she couldn't. She belonged to another man now. She'd given her word.

As if he sensed her inner turmoil, Sean came up behind her. He put his arm around her shoulders and drew her and Eli close. Staking his claim. Tucker watched with narrowed eyes, but made no protest. Had she really expected him to? He had no right.

In the past year, she'd welcomed Sean's comfort too many times to count. Hell, she'd *needed* it. There'd been days when she honestly thought she couldn't go on. Sean had always been there for her. He'd been a good friend, though she'd known he wanted to be more. He'd persisted and finally, after the one-year anniversary of Tucker's death had passed, she'd given in.

If she couldn't have Tucker, Sean made a solid choice. Like her, he valued hearth, home and family.

Looking up to find both men watching her, she sighed. For an instant, she compared them. One tall and lean and dark, the other compact, with dirty-blond hair.

She should be happy. Scratch that, she should be ecstatic. Tucker was here, he was alive and she wished she could celebrate his return without a single reservation. Only she couldn't. She glanced at Sean, saw only love warming his gaze, and kept herself still. She'd be fine. They'd all be fine.

She told herself she was not torn. True, everything had changed. Everything. Tucker was alive, and they had a child together. Of course, that would mean some sort of a relationship had to continue between them, for Eli's sake. Nothing more. Tucker had to understand that. She'd accepted Sean's proposal. He was a good man and she didn't want to hurt him.

Eyeing the man she'd once thought she loved more than life itself, she relaxed into another man's embrace and tried to reconcile her conflicted emotions. She'd loved Tucker once, but now she loved Sean, too. Her love for him might be less fiery, less passionate, but as a mother she trusted that the slow, steady warmth would endure for years, rather than flaming out of control in an unguarded moment.

Her choice had been solid, and not made impulsively. Sean would make a good husband, a fantastic father for Eli, who already appeared to love him.

Eli finished nursing and fell back asleep. Moving him to her shoulder, she refastened her bra and shirt before removing the blanket. Gently patting his back, she burped him. When she finished, she moved away, toward the crib.

"I'll be right back," she said softly. "Don't talk about anything important without me." She was only half kidding.

Moving swiftly, she placed Eli back in his crib and got him settled before she turned to face the two men waiting, still standing silently. The atmosphere felt charged with tension. Uncomfortable.

"He should sleep a little longer," she said, trying to start a conversation.

Still, neither man spoke. She looked from Sean to Tucker and back again, feeling as though she was watching a tennis match.

"It's good to have you home," she said to Tucker. He dipped his chin in acknowledgment, but still didn't respond.

"So," Sean said, finally breaking the awkward silence. "About that explanation?"

Expression grim, Tucker headed for the den, then perched on the arm of the sofa. "I don't know where to begin."

Sean leaned forward, looking from Lucy to Tucker. "If you're willing to talk, we'd love to hear what you have to say."

We'd. Lucy caught the possessive pronoun, aware Tucker probably did, too. Again, the not-so-subtle staking of the claim. Or maybe she was just being hypersensitive.

"I've already told Lucy." Running a hand through his dark, unruly hair, Tucker turned away. When he glanced back over his shoulder, the vivid blue of his gaze sent a shiver through her.

Expression surprised, Sean glanced from one to the other. "I guess she can fill me in later. Still, maybe you can give me the short version. Starting with the plane crash. All we were told was that there'd been a crash and all on board were killed. They found your wallet and your cell phone amid the wreckage. Everything else, including any bodies, was burned beyond recognition."

"There was no plane crash. Or, let me put it another way. The plane Carlos and I were on landed safely." Using much less detail than he'd given Lucy, Tucker filled Sean in on his capture and subsequent imprisonment.

Listening as he told the story again, Lucy closed her eyes.

"All right." Sean accepted Tucker's tale without hesitation. "But after the DEA got you out, they must have told you why. Someone had to know why the cartel held you prisoner for so long."

Tucker gave him a long look. "Because they thought I took their money."

This was new. Lucy opened her eyes to see a look pass between the two men. Not good, though Lucy couldn't put a name to it.

"And now you're home." Sean finished the story.

"And now I'm home. Are you disappointed?" Tucker asked smoothly.

Sean laughed, as though he thought Tucker was kidding. "Right. Disappointed? Hell, this is freaking amazing. You could write a book and make a ton of money."

Lucy noticed Sean didn't answer the question. Tucker probably caught it, too.

"The plane crash was a setup," Tucker said finally. He sounded certain. "And no one has been able to explain to me why someone found it necessary to make everyone believe I was dead. It all goes back to this missing money."

"Seriously?" Sean leaned forward again, curiously expectant. "How much money are you talking about?"

Though Tucker spared him a glance, he continued to focus on Lucy. "Ten million dollars."

Sean whistled, clearly stunned.

Shocked herself, Lucy continued to watch Tucker,

unable to keep her gaze from moving over him like a caress. She'd missed him. So damn much.

"Yeah." Tucker shook his head, shaking off the bad memories like a dog shaking off water. "Apparently, the drug cartel was using coffee beans to smuggle drugs. The scent can throw the drug-sniffing dogs off. I was questioned not only by customs agents, but the DEA, FBI and CIA."

"Ten million dollars is a lot of money." Sean raised a brow. "Did they ever find it?"

"Not that I know of." He sounded unconcerned. "I didn't take it. Right now, the money is the least of my problems."

"Really?" Sean cocked his head, sounding intrigued. "I'd think a missing ten million would be high up there on the priority list."

"Maybe if it were mine or even if I knew where it was. Which it isn't and I don't. So no. Their missing money is their problem. I was lucky that the DEA had agents undercover to rescue me. After I got back, I'd heard the Mexican police wouldn't let the US FAA inspectors examine the supposed plane crash. Apparently, the drug cartel controls that area with an iron fist."

"How'd they find you?" Lucy asked, her heart skipping as he turned his gaze on her.

"I don't have any idea. Since I'd already been declared dead, it wasn't like there was a missing US citizen that they knew of."

"Someone went to a great amount of trouble," Sean said.

"They even brought us a box of your effects." Reaching down inside her shirt, Lucy brought forth the ring she'd been wearing on a chain around her neck ever since it had been given to her. "Your college ring."

Fumbling with the clasp, she finally got it open. Removing the heavy ring, she handed it to him. "Here. You'll be wanting this back."

Watching as he slid the ring back on to his finger, she had to struggle to maintain her composure.

"We had no way of knowing," she repeated, feeling absurdly guilty. Which was ridiculous. If there'd even been a single indication that she should have hope, she would have fought the devil himself to find him. Surely he understood this.

Instead, when they'd come to her with news of Tucker's death, she'd fallen apart. Even remembering the worst day in her life brought back the heavy remembrance of her pain, making her feel queasy.

Jerking his chin in a quick nod, almost as if he heard her thoughts and understood, Tucker spoke again. "Obviously our people were misled, too, unless our government was entirely in the cartel's pocket. They only told you what they believed to be true. That I was killed in a freak accident." Pain warred with fury in the rawness of his voice.

She could tell from his voice that he was done, that he wanted this to be enough to make his life go back to normal. And maybe it would have been, if she hadn't gotten engaged to Sean. She'd truly believed him dead. She'd mourned him, felt her life was over, and carried and birthed his child without him.

"I'm sorry," she apologized, aware an apology was all she could give him at the moment.

Gaze still locked with her, he swallowed hard but didn't speak. Finally, he dipped his head in what could have been a nod. "I'm sorry, too."

"You survived. That's what matters." She hoped he could hear the truth in her voice.

"Yes," Sean interjected. "You made it back in one piece."

"Barely, but yes, I did," he agreed. He closed his eyes, as if by doing so he could shut out the images of whatever horrors haunted him.

Standing next to her fiancé, with his arm around her, Lucy still ached for Tucker and longed to comfort him. Of course she wouldn't, she couldn't even as a friend. Things were different now. They'd never be the same again. She wondered if he regretted this as much as she. Doubtful, considering the issues still unresolved when he'd left for Mexico.

Eli chose that moment to let out a wail. Lucy pushed to her feet, waiting to see if he'd continue or—hope springs eternal—go back to sleep. Another loud cry came from the nursery, then another. Eli was awake again, and he never went back to sleep if allowed to cry too long. Which meant they'd all been granted a reprieve. For now.

Giving him one last lingering look through her lashes, she stood. "Eli calls. If you're hungry, there's plenty of food in the fridge. Make yourself a sandwich or something. I'll be right back.

Tucker watched her go. Motherhood suited her. She'd always been beautiful, but now she had a softness about her. The adoration in her face as she gazed at Eli made his chest tighten. Once, she'd looked at him like that.

As soon as Lucy left the room, Sean cornered Tucker. He'd expected it, so he was reasonably prepared.

"What the hell are you up to?" Sean demanded. "Whatever you're really involved in, you'd better not be doing anything that could endanger Lucy and Eli—your son."

Tucker eyed the man who'd been not only his business partner, helping him start the flourishing coffee company from the ground up, but his best friend since childhood. "You should know better than anyone that I'd never do anything like that."

"I don't." Sean's words leached bitterness. "But even I can tell you're not giving us the entire story. When the government people informed us of your supposed death, they also mentioned this drug cartel. If you actually were kept a prisoner, I'm assuming they had a reason to think you had their money, though I can't imagine what that might have been. So why don't you enlighten me?"

"I can't."

"Can't? Or won't?"

His friend's accusatory tone stunned him. "You know me better than that." Shaking his head, Tucker started to walk away. But something—Confusion? Anger? Hurt?—on Sean's familiar face made him stop. "I don't understand why you're acting like this. None of what happened to me was my fault."

"Maybe not, but still…" Sean gave him a hard look. "What are you hiding?"

This time, though Sean was right, Tucker countered with an accusation of his own. "Why are you so suspicious?"

"Because I care about Lucy and Eli, damn it. If you being here jeopardizes their safety, we have the right to know."

As if Tucker was the outsider. Though he tried to pretend it didn't bother him, truth was, it did. Hurt like hell, in fact.

"I'm here because this is my home," he said simply. "Where I used to live, remember? And Lucy was my girlfriend and you were my best friend. And whether you like it or not, Eli is my son. I'm back now. Here to stay. You'd better get used to that."

"You can't live here with her anymore. She's my fiancée now." There. Sean had actually said it. Tucker supposed he should be glad it was all out in the open.

And so it was. Tucker struggled to control the sudden surge of rage. The last thing he'd expected had been to come home to this.

"I realize that," he replied, his tone steady, even, and completely rational.

"Great." Unaware of Tucker's internal struggle, Sean placed a hand on his shoulder. Though he meant to be brotherly, Tucker couldn't restrain himself. He knocked it off.

"Look," Sean said, his voice ringing with disapproval. "There's no need to be like that. Circumstances have changed. Obviously. No matter how you feel about the way things are now, we can still be friends."

"Can we?" Seeing red, Tucker crossed his arms to keep from doing anything he'd regret, like punching Sean in the face. "Tell me this then. What kind of friend moves in on his best buddy's girlfriend?"

Flushing, Sean took a step back. "I've always loved her," he said. "Only as long as you were around, she never noticed me. I saw my chance and took it. You can't blame me for that. It's been a year," he said, shrugging. "You were dead."

"A year is not long enough." Tucker spoke through clenched teeth, trying to keep his rage under control. "Not nearly long enough. What happened to loyalty? To love?"

"Maybe you're asking the wrong question," Sean answered quietly. "Maybe you should wonder what was wrong in the relationship between you and Lucy that made it so easy for her to find solace in my arms barely one year after your so-called death?"

Talk about a knife slipped under the ribs…

Stunned, Tucker could only stare. Sean was right. Lucy should still be in mourning, if she'd truly loved him. She'd gone from "I'll love you forever" to "I loved you for a year and now I've got to move forward with my life."

How easy had that been for her? Had she even mourned him at all? Obviously there must have been some cracks, some flaws that he hadn't seen a year ago. He thought back to their last conversation before he'd left for Mexico and the allure of exotic coffee.

They'd fought about his wanderlust. And, while he'd known she wanted more from him, he hadn't been certain he was able to give it to her. She'd made no secret of her desire to start a family. He hadn't hidden the fact that he didn't feel he was ready.

Now, he couldn't believe how much it hurt that she'd done so without him. She'd moved on. While he was still stuck in the past, running like hell to catch up.

Damn it. Events had once again spiraled out of his control. Lucy and Sean—picturing them together made him feel like the two of them had jointly ripped his heart from his chest and danced on it.

He'd do better to focus on something he could be in charge of. Finding out if he'd been set up, or if his capture and subsequent imprisonment had been simply a huge, cosmic accident.

He was betting on the former.

And there was the missing money. Who had taken it and had they arranged for Tucker to take the fall for them?

Sean still watched him, rocked on the heels of his feet in an adversarial way, as though he thought Tucker might take a swing at him at any moment and he wanted to be ready.

He was right, Tucker thought with grim amusement. Because it took everything he had not to. Taking a deep breath, he ruthlessly pushed his emotions away and got himself under control.

He could do little to change the past. Right now, he needed to focus on the future.

Before being released from their custody, the DEA had given him a decision to make. He'd told them he'd have to think about it. Ironically, finding Lucy and Sean together had helped him make up his mind.

He needed to make a phone call and let them know.

Since he'd been told not to use the landline and didn't yet have a cell phone, he'd have to get out of the house. Pearl Street Mall was just a few blocks away and he knew neither Lucy nor Sean would find it unusual if he said he needed to take a walk to clear his head and help him think.

"I need some fresh air," he told Sean. "Tell Lucy I'm going for a walk."

Sean nodded, making no move to stop him.

Once outside, he took a deep breath. What a train wreck that had been. During his imprisonment, he'd pictured his and Lucy's reunion a hundred, no a thousand times. Never, even in his wildest dreams, had he imagined this.

Out of shape and cursing his body's weakness, he started off slowly toward Pearl Street. He'd barely gone a hundred yards and he found himself out of breath. Once he'd been used to the high altitude, but no longer. The lack of oxygen combined with his still-weak physical state made him take much longer to walk even a single block.

Finally, he reached the crosswalk that heralded the entrance to the outdoor mall. As it was a holiday, Pearl Street Mall was packed with tourists. Most locals avoided the area like the plague on a day like today.

Finding an actual payphone in the cellular age was more difficult than he expected, but finally he located one on the east end.

Punching in a number from memory, he spoke quietly to the man who answered. "I've thought about your proposition and I've decided to do it. Let's set up a meeting and you can give me the particulars. I'd like to get started immediately."

Chapter 3

Still holding their son close to her chest, Lucy watched out the front window as Tucker strode up the sidewalk. She watched as he faltered and nearly stumbled, and ached to go to him, to help him. Her chest felt tight, the back of her throat clogged with emotion. She couldn't cry, wouldn't cry, at least not now, not in front of Sean.

"Are you all right?" Sean asked softly from behind her. Ah, she couldn't hide anything from him, he understood her so well. Not surprisingly, since he'd known her as long as Tucker.

She drew a shaky breath, centering herself before answering. "I think so. This has all been such a shock, you know?"

"I know." Putting his arms around her, he turned her, baby and all, and held her. He smelled faintly of expensive cologne and his button-down shirt felt stiff with starch. He always looked perfectly put together, his sandy-blond hair styled and his khakis pressed. He was Tucker's polar opposite.

Horrified at herself, she pushed the thought away. Sean was, she reminded herself, her rock. Not once through her ordeal had his devotion faltered. He'd been there for her, asking nothing, while she'd mourned Tucker during her pregnancy. He'd held her hand through the Lamaze classes, and attended Eli's birth as her coach. He'd asked nothing from her until after the baby had been born, and then he'd only asked if they could become a permanent family.

When she'd turned him down, she couldn't help but realize the irony. Once, she'd asked the same thing of Tucker, who had turned her away as well.

Sean was cookouts and cocktail parties, while Tucker was camping and football games. Of course they were different. If Tucker had been the sun blazing in the summer sky, Sean was the moon—peaceful, gentle and always there, no matter the season.

Though seeing Tucker again had stirred up old emotions, she couldn't hurt Sean, wouldn't hurt him, not to go chasing after a fly-by-night wisp of a dream.

Still, she couldn't help herself from glancing out the window over Sean's shoulder. Outside, though the occasional car drove past, she saw no one on foot. Once again, Tucker had breezed into her life like a hurricane, and barely an hour after his arrival, he was off and running.

Worse, she could sense he hadn't told them everything. She knew him just that well.

"Tucker seems...different," Sean said, almost as if he'd read her mind. "He's hiding something," he continued, reminding her that he knew Tucker as well as she did. They'd all grown up together, the three best friends their mothers had jokingly called the Stooges. Back in the day, they'd been inseparable.

"He didn't steal the money." She felt the need to defend him, even though Sean probably knew this as well. "Tucker's not the kind of man to steal."

Sean smoothed back her hair. "Who knows what he is these days. A year as a captive would change anyone. And ten million dollars is a lot of temptation."

She shuddered, glad Sean held her so close that he couldn't see her face. "Please. Don't say that. You know him as well as I do. After all he's been through…"

Sean didn't answer, just tightened his arms around her and Eli, holding them close. Like a family.

Then to her horror, her eyes filled. She felt the first tear stream down her cheek and swiped her hand at it. Pushing out of Sean's embrace, she placed Eli, now quiet, in his playpen; she sniffled, trying to regain control of her emotions.

"Lucy? Look at me, please?" Sean's voice, oddly gentle, compelled her to raise her head. But then, as if she couldn't help herself, her gaze slid past him and to the window once again, searching for a lean, broad-shouldered man who should be returning home and wasn't.

That did it. She gasped, powerless to stop it as her eyes filled and the floodgates opened.

Sean pulled her close again and held her while she wept, bless him. Then, when she tried to step away to tidy up, he went and got the box of tissues and instead of handing it to her, carefully and gently wiped her eyes and face as if she was a small child.

"Better now?" he asked.

She nodded, not trusting herself to speak. Again, she

used Eli as an excuse, crossing to the playpen. His bright blue eyes were open, so she turned on the musical duck mobile and placed several brightly colored toys in the baby's line of vision.

"There," she said, once she'd finished. "That should keep him occupied for a little while." Somehow she took a step, and then another, amazed that her shaky legs still supported her. Once she'd reached the couch, she let herself drop into the soft cushions.

"This just doesn't seem real," she said. "I can't believe Tucker's alive."

A shadow crossed Sean's handsome face. "Do you still love him?" he asked bluntly. "Because I'm not willing to be second best now that he's back. I have a right to know."

Of course he did, but the fact that he asked her this right now felt as though he was blindsiding her.

"I…still have feelings for him," she admitted. "But not romantic ones," she hastened to add, as Sean's face fell. "You know I still love him, Sean. Just as you do."

"As a friend," he said, his tone hard. "And somehow I don't think that's the same kind of love that you're talking about. You and he have been together since middle school."

Her gut clenched. "And now we're not."

"You have a child together." Plainly, Sean wasn't about to let this go. "That's bound to bring you closer."

His earnest brown eyes were guarded and full of hope and fear in equal measures. She felt a moment of pity, which she squashed, aware he wouldn't welcome that.

She couldn't blame Sean for feeling threatened. Their engagement was too new, too fragile. He knew how much she'd loved Tucker. The question of whether she loved him still, she couldn't really answer. She'd barely gotten used to the idea of finding him alive.

"I can only tell you what I know. You have to understand that Tucker and I will always share Eli," she answered softly. "But before he left for Mexico, Tucker made it plain he wasn't ready to settle down."

A muscle worked in Sean's square jaw. "What if he is now?"

Smiling sadly at the question, she shook her head. "Think about what you just said. He reappears after a year, learns we believed him dead, and by way of explanation, he gives us this fantastic and almost unbelievable story. Still, I'm willing to accept that, because it's Tucker.

"Then, just as we're all starting to relax and make an attempt to get used to the idea, he tells us he has to go for a walk to clear his head and boom—he disappears. He wasn't even here an hour. And he's gone. Just like always. He hasn't changed." She hoped he couldn't hear the bitter pain in her voice.

For a moment, that baby mobile was the only sound, as they stared at each other across the living room.

"I don't know what else to tell you." She spread her hands. "Right now, just like before, I'm back to taking it one day at a time. I suggest you save yourself a lot of worry and try to do the same."

Sean didn't appear too convinced. Still, he didn't disagree with her statement, which was a sort of forward progress.

"I'm not going to lie to you, Sean. Tucker's reappearance has hit me like a punch in the stomach. I'm not sure what to think or how to act...."

Suddenly, she jumped up, aware she had to keep moving or lose it again. "How about I make us a couple of sandwiches?" she asked brightly. "Just enough to tide us over until later?"

He nodded, apparently willing to let the topic go for now. "Do you still want to go to the fireworks display at Folsom Field?" he asked carefully.

Momentarily taken aback, she didn't answer. On the one hand, any attempt at normalcy would be good. But on the other… Tucker was home. They should celebrate. Reacquaint themselves and get to know one another. Or something. But he wasn't here, so she couldn't exactly ask him what he wanted to do.

Frustrated, she tried to think. She should be happy, ecstatic even. She didn't understand why she felt so much like crying. Worse, she hated that she felt she had to hide this riot of emotion from Sean.

"I don't know," she finally answered. "I guess we'd better wait and see if he even comes back."

And as Sean nodded his head in agreement, she realized that they both had just acknowledged that there was a very real possibility Tucker would not.

Tucker found Connor O'Neill's Irish Restaurant and Pub on 13th Street easily. The wooden floorboards creaked as he walked across them. Taking a seat at the corner of the curved mahogany bar so that he could keep his back to the wall and face the door, he ordered a wheat beer and drank it slowly, savoring the taste and enjoying the icy coolness of the frosted mug.

The restaurant was crowded with an early lunch crowd. Normally, he enjoyed people-watching, but his thoughts kept returning to Lucy. And Sean. Engaged. WTH?

Picturing them together made him feel sick. Still stunned from the revelation that he'd come home to learn he had nothing, he took another long drink of his beer, signaling the bartender for another. Lucy, the woman who'd always claimed he was The One, who'd claimed she'd love him forever, had moved on. Pretty damn quickly, as far as he was concerned.

Part of him couldn't blame her. After all, she'd truly believed him to be dead. She had a baby to look after and, as she'd said, Sean clearly adored both her and Eli.

The other part of him couldn't help but feel something was wrong. She and Sean? They'd been pals for years, for chrissake. Even if Sean had carried a torch for her, as far as Tucker'd been able to tell, they had zero chemistry between them.

So what gives?

The bartender brought his second beer just as he'd drained the first. Accepting it gratefully, he was about to take a drink when movement at the doorway caught his attention.

A man stepped into the bar, so tall he had to duck under the low doorway. Long-haired with an unkempt beard, he would have looked perfectly at home panhandling at the corner. When his clear gaze met Tucker's, the sharp intelligence in his brown eyes contrasted with his appearance. This had to be his contact, the DEA agent he'd come to meet.

Sliding onto the bar stool next to Tucker, the man he knew on the phone only as Finn gave him a curt nod before ordering.

"How'd the homecoming go? It hasn't even been an hour since my agents dropped you off and already you call wanting to meet. What happened?"

Tucker grimaced, not wanting to go into detail. "Things changed while I was gone. Enough said."

Finn nodded. Waiting until the bartender brought the beer, collected Finn's money, and moved off, Finn took a long drink before he replied. "Sorry to hear that. But I'm guessing that's why you wanted to have a meeting."

"Yep," Tucker agreed. "I have a few questions first."

Finn gave a barely perceptible nod. "Go ahead."

"What's your full name?"

"Finn Warshaw." IF the DEA agent was surprised at the question, he didn't show it. "What else?"

"Who has the missing ten million dollars?"

Narrowing his eyes, the other man studied him. "We don't know," he admitted. "But we are aware that the cartel thinks you might have a clue where it's stashed."

"Still?"

Finn nodded.

"I was afraid of that. Are they still searching for me?"

"Yes. At first, they thought you were killed in the shootout. Right now they have no idea where you are. But they will soon."

Tucker clenched his jaw. "I can't be captured again. I barely survived the last time. I'm telling you up front. I'll shoot to kill before I let them take me. Understood?"

A barely imperceptible nod. "Understood."

Taking a deep breath, Tucker leaned closer. "Then I'm in. Tell me what you want me to do."

Finn took a long drink of his beer, then wiped his mouth on the back of his hand. "First thing we need to do is move you out of Boulder. We've got a place set up for you in Niwot."

Stunned, Tucker shook his head. "I just got back. I'd prefer not to leave town."

At his words, Finn's pleasant expression vanished.

"Do you have family here, friends, a girlfriend? Need I remind you how ruthless the cartel is? If they find out you have someone you care about, they won't hesitate to use her against you. You don't want to endanger anyone else now, do you?"

He was right, damn it. He just had to figure out a way to tell Lucy.

"You can always just vanish, if it'd be easier," Finn said.

"Out of the question." Tucker didn't even have to think about that one. "I disappeared once and she thought I was dead. I won't do that to her again. I owe her some sort of explanation."

"Not a good idea. If you say anything, remember that you can't come even remotely close to telling the truth. You can't tell anyone about this operation, understand? If you do, not only do you risk blowing your own cover, but also the agents we have in place now. You could endanger their lives. Do you understand?"

Tucker nodded. Finishing his beer, he stood and pushed back his bar stool. "Give me a couple of hours. Where do you want to meet?"

"How about here? I'll pick you up out front in two hours. Don't be late."

Inclining his head, Tucker headed out the door, hoping that during the walk home, he could come up with an explanation that made sense to Lucy. He didn't want her to think he was abandoning her and his son for a second time. Unfortunately, no matter how he was able to spin it, he knew that was exactly what she'd think he was doing.

Unable to relax, Lucy took to pacing in front of the living room bay window. Obviously humoring her, Sean simply watched, playing with baby Eli.

The first hour seemed to crawl by. At the ninety minute mark, she'd begun to toy with the idea of going in search of him. "He can't just reappear in our lives and then vanish," she said. "Maybe we should go see if we can find him."

Sean shrugged. "He's a grown man. I'm thinking he can do pretty much whatever the hell he wants."

Torn between wanting to agree and wanting to argue, she glanced once more out the window. Her heart leapt in her chest at the sight of Tucker striding down the street toward them.

"He's coming back," she cried, absurdly on the verge of tears once again.

Sean gave her a long look. "Would you like to run outside and greet him?" he asked, sounding annoyed.

She couldn't really blame him. She supposed she'd feel the same, if the situation were reversed. "Of course not." Managing a smile, hoping to ease the tension that had instantly returned, she crossed the room and hugged him. "Don't worry so much," she murmured.

"I'm not worried," he denied instantly. But she could feel tension in the stiff way he held her and she knew he was lying. He must feel really threatened because in the entire time she'd known him, Sean had never lied to her. Not even once.

A moment later, Tucker knocked softly on the front door. Again, she couldn't help but remember how, before he'd gone to Mexico, he would have walked right in. Of course, he'd lived with her then. Now, he couldn't. He'd have to find someplace else to live. Maybe he could stay with Sean.

Tucker knocked again.

"Let him in," Sean said, sounding resigned.

Giving him a quick kiss, Lucy crossed to the door and opened it, finding a desolate look on Tucker's face.

"Are you all right?" she asked, letting her gaze roam over him, still amazed at how much it hurt to do so.

"I'm fine." He smiled, a wan ghost of his former smile, though she thought she saw a trace of warmth lurking in it.

Her heart skipped a beat as his incredibly blue gaze met and held hers. Again, she had to fight the urge to go to him and wrap her arms around him and breathe in his familiar, masculine scent.

Damn.

Flustered, she looked away, only to find Sean glaring at her as though he knew what she'd been thinking. Maybe, she thought guiltily, her thoughts had shown on her face. Tucker had always said she was a horrible poker player.

Tucker, again Tucker. He was all she could think about. It had to be because his sudden and unexpected appearance had been like a return from the dead. A miracle. Once she got over the initial shock, she'd return to normal.

Another glance at Sean, who fairly radiated jealousy and hurt, mixed with anger, told her the sooner the better.

Watching the silent interplay between Lucy and Sean not only made him feel like an outsider, but the underlying emotions puzzled him. Lucy seemed defensive while Sean…acted almost jealous. Of course, he couldn't blame the other man. If the situation had been reversed, he'd have felt threatened, too. Any man would.

Maybe he could ease the tension a bit.

"I'm going to have to leave in a few minutes," he said. "I'm going to go find a place to stay."

Both Lucy and Sean stared at him as if he'd lost his mind.

"Today?" Lucy asked. "It's a holiday. Nothing's open."

"Plus there's no need," Sean put in. "You can stay with me."

This, he hadn't expected. Unless Sean figured he could keep an eye on him better that way.

"Sounds good," he lied, knowing Sean would be easier to convince of his need to live away from Lucy than Lucy herself. Also, if it came down to it, he rather suspected Sean wouldn't actually care if he disappeared for a while.

Lucy would be more difficult to fool. She'd expect him to want to spend time with Eli. Hell, he wanted to get to know his son. Just not yet. He couldn't risk putting the baby in danger.

Once this thing was settled... He shut down the thought, unwilling to think beyond what he had to do. He felt like he had to keep his focus tight if he wanted a chance at succeeding.

Glancing at his watch, he realized he had approximately forty minutes before he had to meet Finn.

Both Sean and Lucy noticed the gesture.

"No hurry," Lucy hastened to assure him, apparently mistaking the gesture for something else. "You just got here. Why don't you sit and talk awhile? We've got a lot to catch up on."

Right. Searching for a way to distract her, he spotted his flat-screen television still occupying center stage. Exactly where he'd put it after he'd purchased it.

"What about my stuff?" he asked Lucy. Before the trip to Mexico, he and Lucy had lived together. "My clothes, my books, do you still have any of it?"

"Of course I do," she answered, instantly distracted and sounding eager. "I've boxed it up and put it in the basement. You're totally welcome to sort through it and move what you want to Sean's."

"Sounds great. I won't do it right now, but as soon as I can, all right?" Unfortunately, he knew he wouldn't be able to go through his things anytime soon. Maybe after this DEA sting was all over. No, definitely after this was all over.

To his relief, she didn't insist he follow her to the basement and begin searching through his stuff immediately.

"Sounds good," Lucy said, shooting a questioning glance at Sean, who gave a slight nod.

Tucker had to clench his teeth to keep from commenting. Sean flashed him a quizzical look as though he sensed something.

Again he glanced at his watch. He had to get going.

"Listen, would you like to go to Folsom Field with us?" Lucy asked, clearly struggling to fill the awkward silence. "The fireworks display starts at dusk, like always."

"It'll be fun," Sean put in, sounding anything but sincere.

"A great way to celebrate your return," Lucy continued.

Staring at her, he knew he couldn't. "I'm not sure taking an infant to a fireworks display would be wise," he said. "You know the noise is bound to scare him. He'll cry, and you'll have to bring him home anyway."

Lucy frowned. "We were going to watch from outside the stadium, where it's not as loud."

He pretended to consider the idea. "I think I'll pass. You two have fun."

As her frown deepened, he realized why. Before Mexico, July 4th had been his favorite holiday. He'd never missed a fireworks display or an excuse to celebrate.

"Things change," he said softly. "You of all people should know that."

She turned away, making him realize he'd once again hurt her, without intending to.

He pushed away the urge to comfort her. Once she thought about it, she'd realize he was right. All she had to do was look at the ring she wore on her third finger.

One final glance at his watch showed him he was running out of time.

"As a matter of fact," he told Sean, keeping his expression pleasant. "I've intruded on you two enough for one day. You go on with your plans and I'll catch up with you later."

Lucy made a strangled sound, but didn't turn around.

"Sounds good." Sean nodded, looking relieved. "Do you have a cell phone?"

"Not yet." Grateful that he'd been given an out, Tucker smiled. "As a matter of fact, that's one of the things I intend to rectify. McGuckin's Hardware is open. I think I'll head over there and pick out a new phone."

Still, Lucy wouldn't look at him.

"Let me write our numbers down," Sean continued. "That way, once you get your phone, you can call us and give us yours."

Pocketing the slip of paper, Tucker again glanced at Lucy before heading toward the front door. "Catch you later," he said to her back. She didn't respond.

Closing the door behind him, he made his escape.

The walk back to Thirteenth Street took about fifteen minutes. He arrived to find the DEA man was already there.

Driving a nondescript, navy sedan that screamed "government issue," Finn waited from a parking spot in front of the nail salon/spa next door to the pub.

Tucker climbed in the passenger side. Neither man spoke until they'd pulled out.

"We're all set up," Finn said. "My undercover guy is already spreading a rumor that you have the money and are ready to talk."

"Ouch." Tucker grimaced. "They're going to want to capture me again."

"We won't let that happen." Finn shot Tucker a glance. "If we can nab the guys at the top of this cartel, we can shut down a bunch of the border violence and stop truckloads of drugs coming into the U.S. through New Mexico and Texas."

"What do you want me to do?"

"For now, very little. Get settled in your new house, go shopping, and pretend to be scouting out a new location for a new business."

This surprised him. "New business? What do you mean?"

"Since you can't go back to Boulder's Best Brew, at least right now, we've fabricated a story that you're starting up something else. Doesn't matter what, but it doesn't have anything to do with coffee."

"Don't you think we should be a bit more specific?"

"Nah. The drug cartel is gonna realize it's a front anyway. You're looking for some way to launder all that money."

Made sense.

"You guys think of everything." Tucker couldn't help but be glad. If the federal agents were on the ball, that meant the likelihood of the cartel nabbing him was small. He hoped. Because if things started to go south, the DEA wouldn't like what he planned to do.

"Yeah." Finn spared him a tight smile. "With all the stuff that happened with your girlfriend and the guy that used to be your best friend, we're spreading the word on the street that you want out of your partnership in your coffee business."

"If they know about that, then what about my son?" Tucker asked. "Can you guarantee his safety?"

"Your son?" Finn sounded surprised. "You have a kid? That wasn't in my briefing. How old? Where?"

"In Boulder, with Lucy. He's three months old."

"That baby is Sean's," Finn said firmly. "At least, as far as we're concerned."

Tucker started to protest, but Finn held up a hand.

"Sorry. Whether that's true or not doesn't matter, but that's what will keep him safe. Understand?"

Looking out the window, Tucker swallowed back a surprisingly bitter protest. Everything else had been taken from him. Better a lie than cause Eli harm.

"I get it," he finally said, sounding as though he didn't care. "Works for me."

As long as they caught the bastards who were behind destroying his life. That's all that really mattered.

Chapter 4

"He's not coming back." Lucy tried to keep the sorrow and fear from her voice, only half succeeding.

"Sure he will." Sean didn't even sound convinced. "Why wouldn't he?"

"Do you really have to ask?"

"Lucy." Sean put his arm around her shoulder. "Stop trying to read something into nothing. He's glad to be home."

"He has no home," she protested. "He knows we can't live together anymore, he and I. He has nowhere to live, other than with you."

"He'll find a place. And he'll definitely be back, even if just for Eli. He has a son now."

And he didn't have her. They'd been so close and she'd never hidden how much she'd adored him. How could Sean not understand how much that had to hurt Tucker?

As she struggled to form a reply, she caught a glint of something in Sean's expression and she realized she'd misunderstood. Sean did realize, and felt jealous and threatened. He apparently found it easier to pretend no problem existed at all.

Maybe his was the right approach. It would be kind of weird to argue with your current boyfriend about your former.

Except there was Eli to consider. It would break what was left of her heart if Tucker refused to have anything to do with his own son.

Once, she wouldn't have said he was that kind of man. Now, she realized she didn't really know him at all.

"I think we should go ahead with our plans," Sean said, kissing the side of her neck, making her start. "After all, it is the Fourth of July."

"I don't know…" Lucy couldn't think. Actually, the last thing she felt like doing was attending the fireworks display without Tucker.

Then, as Sean eyed her, she realized she'd better get used to doing things without Tucker. She'd made her choice. From this point on, she'd be living the rest of her life without him.

Amazing how that still hurt, in a completely different yet frighteningly similar way than it had when she'd thought him dead.

Tucker was alive, Tucker was home, and she belonged to another man. One who, she reminded herself, she also loved very much.

Finally, she gave in and agreed to continue with the plans they'd made before Tucker's miraculous return.

Working side by side, they made ham sandwiches and packed them in a cooler along with the store-bought potato salad, some paper plates and plastic cutlery. Lucy added a couple of bottled waters and they were nearly ready to go.

First, she had to slather Eli, as well as herself, with sunscreen. Sean helped get her back, then watched while she quickly packed a diaper bag.

Because of the holiday, getting anywhere near CU meant braving crowds, both locals and tourists. Luckily, they didn't plan on actually going inside Folsom Field. Instead, they spread their blanket on one of the grassy hills outside, along with several other families, and enjoyed their picnic. People talked and laughed, played Frisbee and strummed guitars, the fine weather and air of excitement adding to the experience while everyone waited for darkness to fall.

In the companionable summer noise around them, Lucy managed to relax for the first time in hours. If not for the angry vibes Sean continued to radiate, she would have put her head in his lap and let herself doze off in the warm sunlight. Instead, she sat next to him on the blanket, his hip bumping hers, their shoulders occasionally touching, and wished she could think of a way to make his stiff posture relax. She knew he was still thinking about Tucker and what his return might mean to their relationship. She wished he would stop, at least for the rest of the day.

But she didn't know the right words to reassure him— how could she, when she didn't know how to placate herself. This was, she thought, the first time ever that she'd been uncomfortable with Sean. Worse, she really couldn't blame Tucker's return for all of the tension between her and Sean. She believed she'd managed to keep her conflicting emotions about him hidden. Sean's tightly wound demeanor was due to his own issues with the return of her former boyfriend. And those he'd have to resolve himself.

Luckily, she had Eli to distract her. He was slightly restless, and she sang to him in a low voice, rocking and cuddling him. Attempting to keep her infant son happy kept her both from focusing on Sean's patent misery, and her hidden worry over Tucker.

Finally, the sun slipped behind the mountains and darkness began to descend. An air of hushed expectation fell over the crowd. Glancing at Sean, who appeared to have actually been on the verge of nodding off, Lucy looked down to see that Eli had also fallen asleep.

Sean's gaze followed her. He smiled.

"He's asleep," she whispered, smiling back.

Sean nodded, then whispered. "Do you think the fireworks will scare him?"

"I don't know." She'd taken care to make sure Eli was exposed to all the normal sounds of everyday life, but this was louder than normal. "Hopefully not. He's a pretty strong sleeper, but still… What do you think?"

"He'll wake up," Sean said confidently. "As soon as the first one is set off, he'll start crying. Wait and see."

Since he was probably right, Lucy grimaced. "If he does, we'll have to leave."

"I know."

Finally, full darkness. The crowd went silent, waiting. First came a loud crackle from inside the stadium, then one pop after another, boom, boom, boom as a multicolored sparkle of lights filled the sky.

People oohed and aahed and cheered. Meanwhile, Lucy watched her baby. Squirming in her arms, Eli jerked, scrunching his tiny face in preparation for a cry.

"He's not going to go for it," Lucy said, attempting

to soothe her son with soft sounds and light touches. Fussy, he squirmed and then finally let out a loud cry.

"Told you." Sean sounded smug. And annoying.

"Let's go. We've got to get out of here." Standing, Lucy pushed away her irritation with Sean and focused on her son, trying not to panic as another round of fireworks exploded overhead. "I don't know why I thought this was a good idea. I don't want Eli to be traumatized."

"Plus his crying will ruin it for everyone else," Sean put in, gathering up their cooler and blanket while the next set of fireworks went into the sky, detonating above them.

While Sean had a point, Lucy was more worried about her son. "Shhhh, shhh," she crooned, as Eli let out a second loud wail.

"Come on, I'll lead the way." Sean took off, letting her and Eli bring up the rear.

Boom, boom, a cornucopia of colors continued to unfurl in the velvet blackness of the sky. Eli continued crying in earnest. People sitting nearby began shooting them annoyed looks.

"Sorry, sorry," Lucy apologized, struggling to catch up with Sean, who was blazing his way back to the parking lot. This infuriated her, though she tried to suppress her anger, aware both of their emotions were fragile today.

By the time she reached the car, he had the cooler loaded, the engine started and the back door open for her to put Eli in his car seat. She buckled her still-crying baby in, still fighting her irritation with Sean, aware that at least part of it stemmed from comparing him to Tucker.

Tucker would never have left her, carrying a wailing infant, to pick her own way among an increasingly hostile and sometimes inebriated crowd. While she didn't know if he would have taken Eli from her and tried to console him while carrying him high above everyone, she liked to think he would have.

Hell, once Sean would have also. Just not today. She didn't like that he'd taken out his frustration about Tucker on her and Eli.

Once she had the baby secure, she climbed into the passenger side and buckled herself in. As soon as she did, Sean put the car in drive and drove away without speaking. Eli continued to wail, but soon the insulation and motion of the car turned Eli's cries into whimpers, then hiccups, before he fell asleep.

"Finally." She let her breath out in a whoosh.

"Do you want me to drive around for a while?" Sean asked, shooting Lucy a small smile.

"Please," she answered. Then, because her terse response had been clipped, she took a deep breath, trying to let her frustration go.

"You're upset with me," Sean said, his tone conciliatory. Then, before she could answer, he reached over and awkwardly patted her shoulder.

"I'm sorry," he apologized. "I know I didn't help you at all back there, and I'm sorry. I just couldn't…"

Though she knew what he meant, that he couldn't stop worrying about the consequences of Tucker's return, she simply nodded without finishing his sentence as she normally would.

Since she didn't say anything, Sean, too, fell silent. They drove around Boulder, finally taking the Diagonal Highway into Longmont. Once there, he turned around at Main Street and headed back home, Eli still sleeping peacefully, the scary fireworks display apparently forgotten.

Staring out the window, Tucker tried not to think of Lucy and his son, Eli, with Sean. Instead, he squinted west through the darkness, imagining the fireworks in Boulder and trying to remember how much he'd always loved them. Now, the thought of Lucy watching them with Sean's arm around her totally negated any pleasure he might have felt at the celebration.

Twenty minutes later, Finn turned off the Diagonal and headed east, toward an older neighborhood. They pulled up in front of a small, single-story, frame house. The landscaping was well-maintained, the wood freshly painted a pale cream. A "Sold" sign sat square in the middle of the front yard.

"What's this?" Tucker asked, surprised.

"Your new house," Finn said. "If anyone checks the paperwork, you just paid cash and the deed is in your name."

Impressed with the DEA's thoroughness, Tucker got out of the car, following Finn to the front door. Once he'd unlocked the door, Finn handed him the keys. "Here you go."

Inside, the place had been sparsely furnished, though it managed to feel homey. A small sofa, one chair, a coffee table and a fair-sized, off-brand flat-screen TV filled the living room.

"Looks like a bachelor pad," Tucker said, thinking about the apartment he used to have before he'd moved into Lucy's house with her. His living room had been similar to this, but with one exception. He'd bought a top-of-the-line, sixty-inch plasma TV, the same one that now occupied a place of honor in Lucy's den.

She could keep it. Just as well. He wouldn't have had the heart to ask her to return it.

"Go ahead." Finn gestured. "Check the place out. There's new carpet and appliances. We've stocked the pantry and the refrigerator. I'm supposed to stay and make sure I answer any questions before I leave."

"What about cash? I'll need access to my bank accounts."

"We're working on that," Finn said. "We should have your accounts unfrozen in a few days. A week tops. In the meantime, here's a temporary credit card. It's got a two-thousand-dollar limit, so spend it carefully. Consider it a payment for your help in this operation."

Tucker nodded and pocketed the credit card. "What about transportation?" he asked. "Back in Boulder, I had a Harley and a Jeep. Any chance you can find out what happened to them?"

Pulling a small pad of paper from his pocket, Finn made a note. "I'll check on it and get back to you. In the meantime, I was authorized to let you have my car. I can arrange for someone to pick me up."

"No." Tucker told the other man. "That thing screams 'cop'. I'll wait and see if they can bring me my own vehicles. Otherwise, I'll need to pick up something at a used car lot."

"We'll take care of it." Finn didn't sound happy. "In the meantime, I hate to leave you here without a car, so are you sure you don't want to take mine?"

"I'll be fine."

"There's an old mountain bike in the garage," Finn said, tersely. "I guess you can make do with that for now."

He'd used to be an avid cyclist. Before. But then, he thought ruefully, he'd been a lot of things, before.

"Works for me."

"Here." Finn handed him a cell phone. "It's also in your name. You have unlimited minutes and text messages. My number is already in your phone book, under F. Call me if you need anything."

"I will." Taking the phone, Tucker dropped it into his pocket. "Now what?"

"Now we wait for someone to contact you. Don't worry, we've got eyes on the house. No one will be able to get to you without going through us."

Pretending to be relieved, Tucker forced a smile. "Glad to hear it." He cleared his throat. "What about a weapon?"

"No." Finn didn't even hesitate.

Doggedly, Tucker continued. "I need some way to protect myself. Like a gun."

"We'll always be near you. There's no need."

Seeing that Finn wouldn't be swayed, Tucker shrugged. With the area's avid hunting population, procuring a pistol of his own shouldn't be too difficult. For the first time he was glad of the DEA's prepaid charge card with it's two-grand limit.

"Are you sure you don't need anything else?" Finn checked his watch. "I've got a few things to do before I go on surveillance."

This surprised Tucker. "You have to work surveillance, too?"

Finn shrugged. "It's my operation and we're shorthanded, as always. So I help where I can."

"Looks like I'm set," Tucker said. "I'll see you later."

"Probably tomorrow." With that, the DEA agent left.

Once he heard the car start and drive away, Tucker checked out the rest of the house, glad he didn't have to continue to pretend an interest in furnishings and such. To his surprise, the closet had been stocked with clothing in his size, as had the dresser drawers. Jeans and T-shirts mostly. There were even socks, underwear—both boxers and briefs—and shoes. All in his size. Someone had certainly done their research. Scary, but that was under-cover operations for you.

Wandering back to the kitchen, he found the refrig-erator full of food, along with a six-pack of Coors, his favorite beer.

Of course. They'd taken care of everything, right down to the last detail. Pretty soon he'd stop being surprised.

"Thoughtful," he murmured, popping one open and taking a long swallow. He'd see what was on TV and then he'd try and get a decent night's rest in the brand-new bed on the clean, crisp sheets.

In the morning, all bets were off. Sorry, Finn. But there was no way he was going to wait around like a sitting duck or, as he preferred to think about it, bait on a hook. He had his own plan, and they'd have to adapt and provide backup. That was simply the way it was going to be. Finn would learn that soon enough.

As the temperatures rose, nearly setting a record for the hottest day in July ever, Lucy couldn't contain her restlessness. Two more days passed without Tucker reappearing or even calling. Sean reported that he'd never checked in at Boulder's Best Brew. This was so weird and out of character for the Tucker she knew, that her nagging sense of worry and unease intensified.

"Something's happened to him," she told Sean.

"There's no way he'd show up and then disappear like this."

"I'm sure he's fine." Dismissing her fears with a kiss on the forehead, Sean seemed distracted. "Actually, I'm glad he didn't make it into work. Some weird, menacing-looking man came looking for him."

She froze. "What? Who was he? What did he want?"

"I don't know what he wanted." Sean frowned. "Even I was put off by him. Big Hispanic guy, claiming he only wanted to talk to Tucker, no one else. He gave me his card. He claims to be with the Mexican Consulate."

"That could be a good thing."

"No, it's not. I'd bet you he has something to do with that drug cartel and the missing ten million dollars."

Stunned, she stared, unable to mask her fear. "Do you really think so?"

"Yes, I do." Sean seemed absurdly satisfied to relay this information. Sometimes, she didn't understand his thought process. While he might feel a bit threatened by Tucker—who'd gone MIA and wasn't a threat at all—she couldn't believe he'd seriously wish his friend harm.

"The drug cartel? You think he works for them and he's here because of the missing money?"

"The very same one. Of course," Sean hastened to elaborate. "I don't know that for sure. I'm just speculating."

Instead of relieving her, this comment stressed her out even more. "Seriously? But those guys are all on the border, and in New Mexico and Texas and California. What would he be doing in Colorado?"

"Looking for Tucker? Remember, ten million dollars is still missing."

"Surely they've figured out by now that he doesn't have their money. And maybe that guy really was with the Mexican Consulate. Maybe the Mexican government wants to offer their help."

"I don't know." Sean seemed to be relishing his line of thought. "It's possible, but highly unlikely. If this guy really is on the up and up, he would have contacted the DEA or some other office authority. I'm pretty sure he was with the cartel."

"If he was, I don't understand why they still think Tucker took their money. I mean, come on. Wouldn't he have taken off to the Bahamas or the Virgin Islands or something?"

"I don't know. It looks bad, especially with Tucker disappearing like he has. They might still be watching him. His vanishing act makes it more likely that he knows where the money is."

"If this is what they really think…" She hated to voice her fears, but knew she had to. "Then we have to consider the possibility that he's been captured again. We should alert the authorities."

"Honey." Sounding amused, Sean massaged her shoulders. "Tucker is my oldest friend—"

"Then act like it," she snapped, before she could help herself.

Sean narrowed his gaze and cocked his head. "Lucy, come on. You're really upset about this?"

"Of course I am." Moving away, she glared at him. "And I can't believe you're not."

He looked down, and then raised his head to meet her gaze. "Okay, I've got to tell you the truth. Honestly, I find Tucker's story about being held captive…well, slightly off. Think about it. It's crazy."

"Crazy?" Stunned, she sucked her breath in. "I can't believe…you think he was lying?"

"Maybe. Or embellishing the truth. Either way, don't tell me you didn't sense that he wasn't telling us everything."

"You know better." She swallowed back a flash of anger. "Tucker doesn't lie. He might have omitted some details, but he wouldn't lie, especially to us."

Sean shook his head, his brown eyes radiating anger. "Listen to yourself. How can you defend him when you really don't know where he's been and what he's done?"

"He's done nothing. Except show up and then vanish." Close to tears, she struggled to maintain her composure. "I do know him, Sean. No matter what you think, he wouldn't abandon his son."

"No, maybe he wouldn't." Sean grimaced. "At least not permanently. But you have to realize, whether he's innocent or not, he's lying low until all this blows over. Once the cartel goes away, he'll surface again."

Since he held out a branch of hope, she grabbed it and held on with both hands. "Will they? Will the cartel give up and go away?"

"It's possible." He grimaced. "But only once they find their money. Judging by what's been going on at the Texas, New Mexico and Arizona borders, these drug cartels are ruthless and appear to have no fear of repercussions, so whoever took it might give it up, if pressured enough."

"I understand why Tucker might be hiding from them," she said slowly. "But why us? We're his closest friends."

"I'm thinking this may be temporary. Until he gets over the shock of us being engaged, right now, we're not exactly his favorite people. I'm imagining he's pretty damn angry."

"Because we got together?" she scoffed, trying to ignore a twinge of guilt that told her Sean might be right. "Tucker understands." She hoped.

"Does he? I think you're being a bit naive here."

His condescending tone served as a red flag. Worse, she felt certain he knew this and was purposely pushing for a fight to clear the air. The way she felt at the moment, she wasn't sure that would be a good idea. She might say things they both would regret.

Taking a deep breath, she tried to keep her tone rational. "Sean, I know Tucker, even better than you do. We were together a long time. No matter what, Tucker wouldn't make up a story about being held captive to explain away his absence."

"Are you sure about that?" His mouth twisted bitterly. "Or are you letting yourself believe it because having a valid reason makes you feel better about his abandoning you?"

He *was* pushing for a fight. Well, he would have to wait. Refusing to let go of the rest of what she wanted to say, she doggedly pushed on. "Furthermore, if Tucker had ten million dollars, he wouldn't keep it hidden. He has plenty of his own money, you know."

"His funds are all tied up in probate. To regain access, he's going to have to contact the court and prove he's alive. So far, he's made no effort to do that." Sean shook his head. "Which, unfortunately, further proves my point."

"No, that proves nothing except that money means little to him."

Sean threw up his hands. "Come on, Lucy. He needs money to live, just like the rest of us."

To this, Lucy said nothing. She didn't have a good explanation, but damned if she was going to let Sean tar Tucker's reputation with such a wide brush.

Because, when it came down to it, Sean would never change her mind about Tucker. She would never believe he would lie, cheat and steal the way Sean seemed to.

Which proved that on this, they would never see eye-to-eye. Using a technique she'd learned in therapy, she closed her eyes and visualized letting go of her anger. Picturing a bright red balloon floating away, she took several deep breaths, waiting until she felt calm again before opening her eyes.

"I guess you're right," she lied calmly, even managing to give Sean a small, tight smile. "But you know me. I can't help but worry."

"Well, stop." Sean seemed relieved, too. "Maybe you should focus on planning our wedding. That would be the perfect distraction from all of this. The first thing we need to do is choose a date."

Her first reaction—honestly? Horror. Her chest felt tight and she couldn't breathe. Though she realized what Sean was trying to do, she couldn't believe his bad timing.

"Not today," she said, her voice short.

"Then when?" he persisted doggedly.

She couldn't meet his gaze. "Another time, okay? Not today."

Sean put his hand under her chin, lifting it to make her look at him. "I understand," he finally said, his expression telling her he really didn't.

As he moved away to grab a beer from the fridge, she let her thoughts return to what really mattered to her right now. Tucker. She couldn't take much more of this not knowing if he was all right. And then she realized what she'd have to do.

If Tucker was staying away because he was devastated due to her and Sean's engagement, she had to make things right. She had to find him somehow and insist that they talk things out. He was Eli's father and she wanted to make sure he had a great relationship with their son. Nothing more.

Resolve strengthened, she went to check on Eli before getting ready for bed. She bent over him, inhaling his sweet baby smell, before straightening. She had the most absurd urge to see his beautiful eyes, the exact same blue as Tucker's.

Odd how she could miss him as much now that he was alive as she had when she'd thought him dead.

Chapter 5

Waking up the next morning, Tucker felt disoriented. He sat up in the unfamiliar bed, heart pounding, panic clogging his throat as he tried to figure out his location.

Once he'd ascertained he was no longer in the fetid cell in Mexico, he took stock of his surroundings as his memory quickly returned.

Then, stretching, he pushed back the sheet and got out of bed, padding to the kitchen to start the coffeepot. He'd had to grin when he found a bag of Boulder's Best Brew in the pantry. The DEA agent who'd stocked the place must have known better than to buy Folgers or Starbucks.

While the coffee brewed he poured himself a bowl of cereal with two percent milk. He didn't normally eat cornflakes, preferring Cheerios, but he'd make do with what he had. After Mexico, he found himself much less particular about what he ate.

Everything tasted like ambrosia, which meant his recovering body was still starved for nutrients.

Breakfast finished, he downed his first cup of coffee as quickly as possible, needing the caffeine jolt. The second cup he savored, walking from room to room. The little house provided by the DEA felt sterile and as far from his home as possible, but at least it felt safe.

Still, damned if he was going to sit here like a minnow on a fishhook, waiting for the cartel to come and try to kill him.

Instead, he'd have to decide on a plan of action.

He started with the obvious. If the DEA had made sure that word on the street was that he was back in Colorado, then if the cartel was searching for him, they'd begin with his business.

Ergo. He'd stake out the offices of BBB—Boulder's Best Brew.

Riding his bike back into town, he stopped and bought a pair of dark sunglasses at the drug store, along with a fake beard he found, inexplicably in the toy section.

Then, glad McGuckin's Hardware store opened at 7:30, he roamed the clothing area and grabbed a green cap with the words "John Deere" printed on it, a pair of denim overalls with the McGuckin's logo embroidered on the pocket, which he paired with work boots and a long-sleeved, button-up work shirt. After he paid for his purchases, he changed in the men's room and studied himself in the mirror. With the fake beard in place, he almost didn't recognize himself.

Satisfied that he looked as different from the CEO of BBB as he could get, he put on his new sunglasses and rode the beat-up mountain bike down Arapahoe. Glad of Boulder's fantastic bike areas, he made better time than the traffic.

At the sight of the two-story, brick building he leased, he felt nostalgic. Parking his bike in the bike rack, he sauntered toward the corner café where he marketed his coffee.

Glad to see a small crowd queued at the counter, he got in line. He purchased a large latte, slightly amazed and gratified that no one recognized him. On the way out, he bought a copy of the *Daily Camera* from the newsstand, and stationed himself on the brick wall, near the corner where he could see everyone coming and going from the BBB corporate offices.

Watching as his employees arrived for work felt oddly bittersweet. One by one, he recognized them with a sense of shock akin to joy. First to arrive was kindhearted Aida, his fifty-something personal assistant, who liked to pretend she still lived in the seventies. She always wore tie-dyed blouses with vintage bell-bottom jeans. Today she'd paired this with a matching headband.

Right behind her came Phil Pilling, the pompous director of marketing, wearing neatly pressed chinos with a starched button-down shirt. Phil drove a battered BMW and always managed to figure out a way to drop high-end, name brands into any conversation.

During the next twenty minutes, Tucker watched as various clerical employees arrived. He was on a first-name basis with many of them due to his predilection of dropping by the various departments unannounced and visiting with the staff. Even so, not a single one spared him a glance.

But then, as far as they all knew, he was still dead. Though he told himself it was all for the best, at least until he'd brought his captors to justice, he'd never realized until this very moment how much he'd missed them.

Finally, at exactly eight-thirty, the last stragglers arrived at work and his building entrance grew quiet. Meanwhile, the BBB coffee shop he'd put on the westward corner had a steady stream of customers. Even though it was a workday for the locals, tourists still packed Boulder in the summer.

Sipping his cooling coffee, he settled in to wait. Once he'd skimmed the entire newspaper, he set that down and concentrated on drinking the last of his coffee. That done, he people watched, amusing himself by picking out the tourists from the locals.

After an hour of this, he realized that, contrary to what television portrayed, stakeouts were boring. As the sun climbed the sky, the temperature rose and he moved to the shade. Despite the fact that he'd gotten a good night's sleep, he found it more difficult to keep his eyes open than he would have believed.

Finally, he got up and purchased a second cup of coffee and a bagel. As noon approached, he switched the coffee for a can of diet soda. Luckily, his shop sold sandwiches, so he figured he'd just grab one of those for lunch.

Only a few people entered or exited his building. Since the employees were already at work and the delivery entrance was at the back, watching the front door had become an exercise in monotony. Since he didn't have anyone to relieve him or provide backup, he could only hope nothing happened on the rare occasions he had to leave his post.

When the dark-skinned man appeared at one o'clock, Tucker had just returned from the men's room and almost missed him. Frequently glancing at a notepad, black hair styled impeccably, the man stopped in front of the building and stood back, staring up at the sign. Wearing a dark suit and tie, he looked out of place in free-spirited Boulder, where even CEOs like Tucker frequently wore jeans, sandals and T-shirts.

Appearing to finally reach a decision, the man entered the BBB building. Through the sparkling clean glass, Tucker could see the reception desk where the man stopped, apparently to ask directions before getting into an elevator. Tucker wondered if Sean was about to have a visitor.

Though the man looked Hispanic, that didn't mean he was a member of the Mexican drug cartel. Still, Tucker didn't believe in coincidences. Adrenaline pumping, he fidgeted but forced himself to remain still and exercise patience. Ten minutes later, he was rewarded as the man exited the building and began walking, heading toward Fourteenth Street.

On foot. What could be better?

As he fell into place behind his target, Tucker noticed another man, casually dressed, doing the same. Was he DEA surveillance? Or had his enemies spotted him? Were they closing in, leading him into a trap?

Telling himself to stop being paranoid, he continued to follow, taking care to keep other people between them.

When they reached one of the many small parking lots, the man cut across and unlocked a red Ford Explorer, climbing in. Tucker kept walking, aware he couldn't follow now.

The third man, still a good fifty yards behind Tucker, also stopped, appearing torn. Then, apparently coming to a decision, he continued on toward Tucker.

"Other agents will follow him," he said sotto-voice

as they passed each other. "You're not supposed to even be in Boulder. You need to get back to the safe house, where you belong."

DEA then. Both relieved and dismayed, Tucker grimaced, plastering a fake smile on his face. "How did you recognize me?"

The other man shot him a quizzical look. "You've been followed since you left the house."

"Good to know. But I'm just enjoying the sunshine."

"In disguise? Right. Whatever. Finn will be contacting you shortly," the agent continued. "But be aware that if you want our protection, you've got to do as we say."

"And therein lies the problem."

The other man stared at him blankly. "What?"

"Never mind." Shaking his head, Tucker continued to walk. "I'll take it up with Finn when I talk to him. Right now, I'm going to go have a beer. Want to join me?"

"Can't." For the first time the DEA agent cracked a smile. "I'm on duty. Maybe another time."

Lifting his hand in a wave of acknowledgment, Tucker headed for Connor O'Neill's. He'd have a beer and some wings before grabbing his bike and pedaling back to his house.

Eli had a doctor's appointment today, so Lucy headed up to the medical office on Broadway. She was running early, so as she often did for no reason, she drove by the BBB corporate office, planning to pick up a cup of coffee, if the drive-thru wasn't backed up.

Sometimes she dropped in to meet Sean for lunch, but it was twelve-thirty and he would have already eaten. He liked to have his midday meal at exactly noon. Since

Eli's pediatrician appointment was at one and she liked to be a few minutes early, she didn't even have time to pop in and say hello, even if Sean had only grabbed a quick sandwich to eat in his office.

Not that she really wanted to. Things had been different between the two of them since the Fourth of July. It was like Tucker's specter hovered over him, which was made worse since he wasn't even dead.

But it sure felt like he was, she thought bitterly. He hadn't returned after he'd left the second time, not even to stay with Sean as he'd claimed he wanted to do. Nor had he called to give them his new cell phone number. For all intents and purposes, she might have dreamt his return.

Except she hadn't. And that made his disappearance hurt even more. Especially since he now knew he had a son. And that upset her most of all.

She could understand that seeing her with Sean bothered him. She could definitely sympathize. But to totally ignore Eli, his own son? That made the mama bear in her come out, claws ready.

Since the BBB coffee shop drive-thru had four cars waiting, she decided to pass. Going inside would involve not only locating a parking space, but unstrapping Eli from his car seat, gathering up all the apparatus that traveling with a baby meant. Too much effort for an early afternoon jolt of java.

Still, she couldn't resist cruising slowly by. Though Sean was a partner in the business, BBB had been Tucker's brainchild and she thought of him whenever she saw the logo, three intertwined, stylized Bs.

The coffee shop had settled down a bit from the normal morning rush, though every outside table was full as customers sat on the patio enjoying their caffeine fix and the warm sunshine. As she drove by, she eyed them, nearly doing a double take as she drove further down the street and one man caught her eye. Striding away, his broad shoulders and the tilt of his shaggy head brought a jolt of recognition to her stomach.

Tucker?

Could it be? But no, a second look revealed this man had a bushy black beard, and wore denim coveralls and a green and yellow John Deere cap, something Tucker would never do. Actually, the man had the look of a farmer on a day trip to the not-so-big city. Still, the resemblance was uncanny enough to make her catch her breath. Too bad his sunglasses had hidden his eyes. Tucker's bright blue eyes would have been a dead giveaway.

Great, now she was seeing Tucker everywhere, even in total strangers. Still, she couldn't erase the feeling that she'd missed something.

Chest aching, she continued on to Eli's doctor appointment. It was for his three-month checkup and she didn't want to be late.

The folks at the doctor's office adored Eli and for his part, he appeared to take all this adulation in stride. He smiled and made bubbles as they cooed over him, and didn't even cry once until it was time for his shot.

Watching his perfect little face go from genial happiness to shock, then turn red as he began crying his little heart out, Lucy actually got tears in her eyes.

Evidently used to the reaction of young mothers with their first babies, the nurse smiled and squeezed her shoulder before handing her a strawberry sucker.

An hour later, exiting the medical building, even though she told herself not to, she drove by the BBB building again and searched the streets near the café.

The man was gone—he could have gone anywhere, so she chalked it up to an overactive imagination and went on home.

After enjoying his beer and some super-hot wings, Tucker got up to go. He wasn't looking forward to the long bike ride back on the Diagonal Highway out to Niwot. But he knew better than to hang around Boulder. Though everyone he'd known, except Lucy and Sean, still believed him dead, he still stood a higher chance of being recognized here, in the town where he'd had both his home and his business.

He thought again of the man in the red Ford Explorer, wondering who he'd been and what he'd wanted. Would the DEA even tell him if they learned anything about him? He doubted it. As far as they were concerned, Tucker was simply bait, placed to lure their target.

That, he didn't like. While he welcomed their help—after all, they had much better resources than he did—he wanted them to back him up rather than the other way around.

Since he knew Finn and the people he worked for would never agree to this, he'd have to figure out a way around it. In the meantime, he'd continue to investigate to the best of his ability.

Pedaling a bike usually invigorated him. Today though, with temperatures in the mid-nineties and having consumed a beer, he got dehydrated by the time he reached the IBM plant. He wheeled into a gas station and went inside to purchase a large bottle of water. On the way back to where he'd left his bike, he spotted the pay phone and realized what he needed to do. He needed to make the call he'd been putting off all week.

Since he didn't want Sean—and especially not

Lucy—to have his cell phone number, calling them from that was out. With caller ID all they had to do was make a note.

No, instead, he could call them from a random pay phone. Them? He shook his head, amused at his own self-deception. Who was he kidding? He had no intention of phoning Lucy. He could well imagine her anger. Plus, Lucy knew him too well. She'd be sure to spot the lie in any explanation he could give, especially since he didn't really have one. On top of that, he could find out from Sean what the suspicious man had been doing at the company.

Pulling the slip of paper from his pocket, he deposited money and dialed the number. Sean answered on the second ring.

"Sean, it's Tucker."

"Tucker?" Sean sounded surprised. "Where the hell are you?"

"I'm safe," he said, resolving to stick as close to the truth as possible. "I've been advised to hide out for a little while."

"Good plan. They're looking for you, man. Some guy stopped in at the office today, asking for you. He was Hispanic and spoke with a pretty thick accent."

A-ha. "Did you get a name?"

"Sure." Sean sounded tired. "Though I'm pretty sure it was fake. He said his name was Miguel Gonzalez, which is only one of the most common Mexican names around."

"True." Tucker wrote it down anyway, just in case.

"He left a card," Sean said, surprising him. "His telephone number is 555-1234. He claims to be with the Mexican Consulate."

Interesting. Such a thing would be easy to verify. And

if he was, that meant the corruption had reached even higher levels than the DEA had first thought.

Or maybe they hadn't shared everything with him.

"Thanks, man," Tucker continued. "I'll give him a call. So…how's everything?"

After a moment of silence, Sean responded. "If by everything, you mean Lucy, she's fine. She's still mad as hell at your disappearing act, but that's mostly because she wants you to get to know Eli."

Hearing the undercurrent of anger in Sean's voice, Tucker knew he should leave it alone. But he couldn't. He hoped Sean would understand.

"Will you give her a message for me?"

Sean didn't answer.

Doggedly, Tucker continued. "Tell her I'll try to see Eli as soon as I can, but it's not safe right now. Will you pass that on for me, please?"

Again the small silence.

"Sure," Sean finally said, a bit begrudgingly. "I'll tell her. Anything else?"

Not "do you need anything" or "is there anything I can do to help" or even "are you all right." Tucker supposed he needed to get used to the fact that he'd lost his best friend.

"Nope, thanks though," he replied, hoping he sounded carefree enough.

Apparently, he did.

"Okay, great. Have a good one." And with that, Sean disconnected the call.

Shaking his head, Tucker replaced the receiver, then rummaged in his pocket for more change. Once he'd deposited the correct amount, he dialed the number he'd written down.

"Bueno," a man answered.

"Miguel Gonzalez?"

"*Sí?* And you are?"

"Tucker Drover."

Miguel's sharp intake of breath revealed his surprise.

"I heard you were looking for me," Tucker continued. "Here I am. What do you want?"

"As a representative of the Mexican Consulate, I'd like to extend an offer of protection to you."

It took every ounce of self-control Tucker possessed not to snort out loud. "You're not with the Consulate. Who are you?"

"My position is equivalent in my country to what the Drug Enforcement Agency is in yours."

Another lie. Still, he had to give the guy props for trying.

"You're with the cartel, aren't you?"

"Do not insult me, *amigo.*"

"I'm not your *amigo,*" Tucker responded. "What do you want?"

Either Miguel Gonzalez or whatever his real name was had no patience, or he knew Tucker had figured out the truth. "You know exactly what I want."

Ah, now they were getting somewhere.

Still, Tucker couldn't resist messing with the guy a little. "Maybe I do, maybe I don't. Enlighten me, just in case I'm wrong."

"Don't toy with us," Miguel snarled. "You have no idea what we're capable of doing to get what we need."

"Oh, but I do," Tucker countered, grim and serious. "You forget that I've already dealt with you people once before."

The other man cursed in Spanish. "How much do you want?"

This startled Tucker and at first he couldn't think of an answer. Miguel took his silence for assent.

"All right. How about $500,000 U.S. dollars? Tell us where the money is and you can have that for a cut."

Tucker couldn't help it—he laughed. "One twentieth? Why in the hell would I take that?"

"It's our money. It doesn't belong to you."

"It does now." Tucker gave a slow, deliberate chuckle. "Deal with that. Let's see, ten million versus five hundred thousand. Hmm. You do the math."

Miguel started to speak, but Tucker cut him off. "You think about it, my friend, and come up with a better deal. I'll be in touch."

Then, while Miguel was still sputtering, Tucker disconnected the call.

Replacing the receiver, he realized his palms were sweating. He wiped them off on his jean coveralls and headed for his bike. Time to get back home and then call Finn and let him know he'd done as he'd been told.

"I thought I saw Tucker today," Lucy told Sean, while she peeled potatoes at the kitchen sink. She'd deliberately chosen that moment to make her statement sound more casual.

Behind her, she could sense Sean going all motionless.

"Where?" Sean asked.

"It wasn't him," she hastened to say. "Just some guy that sort of resembled him. Except this guy had a beard and wore jean overalls and a John Deere cap."

"In other words," Sean said slowly. "The perfect disguise."

She hadn't thought of that. "Why would he need to disguise himself?" Then she gasped as she realized why, gripping the sink. "He's hiding from us. Oh, my God."

"Not from us." Sean shook his head. "From them. The drug cartel."

She stared. "He escaped from them, remember? Are you saying they might have come after him?"

"All I know is what I told you. Some Mexican guy showed up at work, asking for him."

"From the cartel?"

"No. He said he was with the Mexican Consulate," Sean told her. "Which is why I sort of wonder if all this is in Tucker's head."

Lucy rubbed her temple. "Not real? This is too much. Maybe we can ask the FBI or the DEA or whoever?"

"Maybe we can mind our own business," Sean pointed out gently. "Either way, Tucker is convinced someone is after him. If no one is, it'll play out over time and we can make sure he gets help. If the drug cartel really is, then I'm sure he's doing what he thinks is right."

"Maybe. But then why is he avoiding us? Surely he knows we won't betray him."

"No doubt he has his reasons." Sean cleared his throat. "He told me to tell you he'll try to see Eli as soon as he can, but it won't be anytime soon."

"You talked to him?" Shaking, she set down the potato peeler and clasped her hands together to try to hide this. Finally, she turned to face Sean. "Is he all right?"

A look of annoyance flashed across Sean's patrician features. "He sounded just fine. He's a big boy."

"Let me get this straight. Either Tucker is having a breakdown or has PTSD, or the Mexican drug cartel is after him." Hands on hips, she glared at her fiancé. "But you think leaving him to deal with either of these alone is just fine."

"I'm sure he can handle himself." Sean's response sounded weak.

"Not if he has PTSD. He needs to get some help."

"Let's not go jumping to conclusions," Sean cautioned. "There's a very real chance that he is in danger."

"And again, you think he can handle himself. Against the Mexican drug cartel?" Dizzy, she closed her eyes. When she opened them again, she shook her head. "Did you offer to help him? Either way, no matter which scenario is true, did you offer him your assistance?"

Instead of answering right away, Sean watched her intently. Finally, he asked a question of his own. "Did you want me to?"

She didn't understand. "What kind of a question is that? Of course I want you to help him. Why wouldn't you?"

"Because if I did, I might be putting my own life in danger," he said slowly. "And if he really has PTSD, I'm sure he's aware of the possibility and has access to get his own help."

"You didn't answer the question," she said. "Did you offer to help him?"

"No." The answer burst from him. "If he wanted my help, he would ask for it. If the Cartel is after him, I'd be at risk. As would you and Eli. Would you want that?"

He was talking crazy. But at least now she understood why. Once again, his jealousy of Tucker had reared its ugly head, obscuring reason and common sense.

Though she knew she should cross the room and wrap her arms around him, she didn't want to. She had enough to worry about without having to soothe his fears every time Tucker's name was mentioned.

"Stop it." Holding his gaze, she kept her voice quiet, her tone reasonable. "Why are you acting like Tucker is the enemy?"

Now he looked down, flushing. "Because you loved him so much," he finally mumbled. "And I'm afraid—"

"Don't be." Now she did go to him and put her arms around him. "I'm engaged to you, not him. What he and I had is over."

His eyes searched hers. "Are you sure about that?"

She nodded. "Yes. Sean, I asked Tucker not to go to Mexico. You know what, but you don't know why. I told him he was gone too much. I wanted more, and Tucker..." To her mortification, her voice broke.

Clearing her throat, she continued. "Tucker didn't. He promised we'd talk when he got back, but he never returned."

"But he did, Lucy." Pushing out of her embrace, he stepped away. "That's the thing. He's back now. You have a child together. How do I know you and he won't pick up right where you left off?"

"Because of this." She held up her ring finger, flashing her engagement ring at him. "How well do you know me, Sean? Do you really think I'd cheat on you with him?"

He had the grace to look ashamed. "Well, no. But—"

"No buts. Either you trust me or you don't."

"I trust you, Lucy." But he didn't sound certain. "It's him I don't trust."

"I can handle myself," she snapped, raising her voice,

apparently loud enough to wake Eli, who let out a cry. Great.

Taking deep breaths to calm herself, she hurried off to the baby's room. But not before she heard Sean's muttered response.

"That's what I'm afraid of, Lucy. That's exactly what I'm afraid of."

Chapter 6

When Finn returned Tucker's call, he was less than pleased to learn that Tucker had contacted Miguel Gonzalez on his own.

"What the hell were you thinking?"

"Hey, I did what you wanted," Tucker responded. "And now this guy really believes I have their money or at least know where it's hidden."

Finn cursed. "Maybe so, but are you sure he's even with the cartel?"

Tucker answered honestly. "No. He said he was with the Mexican Consulate. But I'm pretty sure he was lying."

"That's easily verified. But even if he is with the consulate, he still could be working for the cartel. There's a lot of government corruption there."

"So what's the problem?" Tucker dragged his hand

through his hair. "I did what I was supposed to do. You wanted bait, you got bait."

"That's not what you were supposed to do," Finn exploded. "How can we keep you safe if you insist on wandering around in disguise? And riding a bike. Which reminds me. We're bringing you a vehicle. Once it gets delivered, you're to use that. And call me before you go anywhere."

Tucker waited until Finn took a breath. "Are you finished?"

"Not quite." Though Finn's tone was still stern, Tucker could hear the smile in the other man's voice. "As to Miguel Gonzalez, I don't know who he is or who he works for. Obviously, that's an assumed name. Give me the phone number and I'll run it. I might even call him. Either way, we need a visual."

"I can provide that," Tucker told him. "Miguel visited the BBB offices today. My security cameras most likely got a good picture of him. Talk to Sean Morey. He's the co-owner."

"He visited the BBB offices?" Finn got quiet. "How do you know this?"

Crap. He decided to go with the truth, or part of the truth. "Sean told me. He said the guy came by looking for me.

"Sean? When did you see him?"

"I didn't. I talked to him today, from a pay phone."

Finn groaned. "You made contact with a civilian. Even though we expressly asked you not to. Does he know you're part of the operation?"

"Of course not." Tucker scratched the back of his neck. "Though I did tell him I was in hiding, that the drug cartel might be looking for me, and that you guys were trying to protect me and catch them."

"Too much information," Finn said with a sigh. "But what's done is done."

"I want Sean to know that much, at least. Just in case those criminals try to mess with him or Lucy. If he's informed, at least he can protect her."

"We've got people watching them as well," Finn admitted. "Just as a precaution."

Tucker's stomach clenched. This meant the DEA was aware there was a possibility the cartel would make the connection between him and Lucy and Eli. "Promise me if your men see the slightest hint that Lucy and the baby are in danger, you'll take them into protective custody."

"Of course," Finn answered. "But I really don't think you have to worry about that. As far as they're concerned, that baby is Sean's child and Lucy is his fiancée. No current ties to you."

"Good."

"Yeah. And Tucker? Let's keep it that way, okay?"

"Of course." This was one area where he whole-heartedly agreed with the DEA. "I won't make any attempts to contact Lucy."

"Or Sean," Finn said. "In fact, the less contact you have with anyone from your old life, the better. There's nothing you can do there. Stay out of Boulder, period."

Tucker thought about telling the DEA agent that he had no intention of doing this and that he was careful. He wore a disguise, just to stay on the safe side. But why borrow trouble? After all, if the DEA had men watching him as they claimed, then Finn already knew this.

"How many people have they sent after me?" Tucker asked.

Finn went quiet, as though debating whether or not

it would be ethical to answer. Finally, he cleared his throat. "Several, but no one high enough to warrant notice. However, I should warn you that rumor has it they're planning to send *El Pescado.*"

"The fish?" he translated. "Who the hell is that?"

"He's their top assassin," Finn told him. "If they send him, we're really going to have to beef up your security. However, I don't think we have to worry about that just yet. You're of more value to them alive than dead, as long as they believe you've hidden their money."

"Right." Tucker grimaced. "By the way, does anyone actually know where this money is stashed?"

Finn paused, and then admitted that he didn't know. He concluded the call with an admonishment to Tucker to stay safe.

Clicking the cell phone off, Tucker went to see if he had any coffee left in the pot. Time to plan his next move.

Unable to shake the certainty that the strangely dressed man she'd seen near Pearl Street Mall had actually been Tucker wearing some sort of odd disguise, Lucy decided to take Eli for a walk in his stroller. When she'd first gone on maternity leave in late April, a week before her due date, she'd walked to the mall every day, hoping to hasten the start of labor. Once Eli had been born, she'd occasionally taken him for strolls, though mostly she'd preferred to explore her own neighborhood.

Now, the mall held much more appeal. Despite Sean's rationale, Tucker avoiding them didn't make sense. Not to her. The idea of him suffering with PTSD haunted her as badly as the thought of him being hunted by ruthless drug lords.

Either way, she couldn't go on with her normal routine

as though Tucker wasn't in trouble. She couldn't stand by and do absolutely nothing, unlike Sean. She had to find him and offer her help. If he then declined, she'd at least know she'd tried. Considering what they'd once meant to each other and that he was the father of her child, Tucker deserved that, at the very least.

Deciding not to tell Sean made her feel vaguely guilty, but she didn't want to deal with the fight that would be sure to follow. While she believed he knew better than to attempt to outright forbid her, she could imagine the accusations, both silent and spoken. No matter what explanation she gave, no matter how true, she knew what he would think.

No, she would not tell him. For all intents and purposes, she was taking her baby out for a stroll on a beautiful summer day.

Outside, the sun blazed down from a cloudless blue sky. She went out to get the mail and gauge the temperature. Hot, but not too bad for a nice, leisurely stroll. As a precaution, she put SPF-45 sunscreen all over Eli's soft, pale skin as well as her own.

Once she had Eli securely buckled in the stroller, with the little top up to provide shade, she walked to the mall, taking her time, trying to enjoy the day. Unable to keep from feeling slightly paranoid, she made sure to check out her surroundings, looking behind her and in front of her, eyeing every house, every driveway. She couldn't shake the feeling that she was being followed.

But she saw no one other than people jogging with their dogs or other mothers taking their own babies for a stroll, so she put down her jitters as a case of nerves. All this talk about drug cartels and torture would make anyone nervous.

After a few minutes, she reached the edge of the

pedestrian shopping center and stopped, taking in the brick walkway with leafy trees shading the center aisle. She loved this place. Every season it took on a different life, switching moods as often as the weather. In the summer, the place was full of tourists and locals, but the usual swarm of college students attending CU was conspicuously absent. In the fall, the harvest decorations matched the changing leaves. At Christmas, she loved to shop here, trudging through the snow and listening as the bells tinkled merrily on various shop doors.

Waiting for the light to allow her to walk, Lucy joined the small crowd crossing the pedestrian path to the mall. Once she'd made it, she let the others pass and pushed the stroller to a shady spot where she could observe quietly.

The usual crowd, an eclectic combination of tourists and residents, mixed with students hanging out over the summer, made the outdoor mall a lively place. Children played in the water fountains, squealing as the water cooled them and laughing as they splashed. At one end of the mall, the requisite guitar player strummed madly, his case open on the ground next to him for donations. At the other end, a saxophone crooned soulfully.

Pretending to be interested in the window displays, most of which had a patriotic theme, Lucy pushed her stroller, smiling and nodding at the numerous other young mothers who were accompanied by their children. Eli dozed, content with the motion of the stroller. The summer day was warm, the sunshine bright. Nothing appeared remotely suspicious or threatening and gradually she began to relax. This was, after all, one of the pulses of her town. If she wasn't safe here, where would she ever be safe?

As she got closer to the BBB building and the

always busy corner coffee shop, her sleepy nonchalance vanished. Heart rate accelerating, she picked up her pace. When she was close enough to do so, she found a shady spot and stopped. From there, she searched the crowded streets for the man who'd so resembled an oddly dressed Tucker.

She didn't see him. Not here or anywhere on this block or the next. Her stomach clenched as she looked again. Nope. He wasn't there.

Disappointment warred, oddly enough, with relief. After all, she wasn't positive it had been Tucker. It might have just been someone who looked like him.

In the unlikely event it had been Tucker, she hadn't been sure what she would say to him if she did encounter him. Though she had a lot to say, she'd prefer to have some discussions in private.

Still… Either way, all she needed was a good look in his eyes. No matter what the disguise, she knew she could recognize Tucker this way. Unless he had put on colored contacts, the extraordinary blue shade would give him away instantly.

Which might explain why the man had worn dark sunglasses. Of course, it was summer and most everyone wore them, herself included.

Canvassing the crowd one more time, she let her shoulders slump as she saw no sign of him. Maybe she should just give up and go home. This subterfuge thing was driving her crazy. Hell, Tucker was driving her crazy. It was as if he wasn't content that he'd been believed dead and had returned just in time to learn of her engagement. Oh, no, now it appeared that he felt the need to mess with her even more.

Oh, she knew he no doubt had valid reasons for his actions, but she couldn't help the way she felt.

Maybe she'd be better off returning home and giving up this crazy idea to find the man from yesterday. Wavering, she slowed her steps, trying to decide.

Her initial plan had been to visit the coffee shop, grab one of the iced coffee drinks and a snack, and try to snag an outside table where she could watch everyone walk by.

This still seemed like a good idea, she decided. She'd come this far and couldn't abandon the idea now. After all, even if the man wasn't here, he could still show up. She wanted a good vantage point if and when he did.

As she approached the corner coffee shop, still scanning the crowd, she spotted him strolling up the street. Wearing the same green John Deere cap, minus the denim overalls, he kept his head down as he hurried toward the same destination as she. Exactly where she'd spotted him yesterday.

Tucker. Oh, my God, he looked so much like Tucker.

Heart pounding, she started toward him, pushing her stroller in front of her. So intent was he on where he was going, he never noticed her or broke stride. Because he once again wore dark sunglasses, she couldn't be one hundred percent positive he was Tucker, but everything from his build to the purposeful way he strode, screamed that he was.

Right before he reached the doorway, she called out his name. "Tucker!"

Instantly, he turned. She could tell the instant he realized what he'd done. By then, it was too late.

"I knew it was you." Catching up to him, she grabbed at his sleeve. "Even with that weird beard thing on, I could—"

"You shouldn't be here," he said, his voice low and

urgent, his expression horrified. "You need to take Eli and get the hell out of here."

Stunned, she could only stare. "But—"

"Now," he snarled, practically shoving her away. "Before someone sees you talking to me and puts two and two together."

"I don't understand." Frozen, she stood gazing up at him, trying to figure out why her heart felt like it was breaking.

"Lucy!" He dragged a hand through his hair in agitation. "The cartel is looking for me. What if you were followed?"

Then, as she could only eye him blankly, he continued. "You don't really understand how dangerous this is, do you?"

"No," she stammered, wondering if he'd lost his mind.

"That's why I'm wearing this disguise." He took a step backward, shaking his head. "Go on now. You have to stay away from me."

She wanted to disagree and indeed, was on the verge of mustering up what she thought was a compelling argument, when he lowered his sunglasses, letting her see his eyes. Fear—no, more than fear—absolute terror shone starkly in them.

"Go away," he repeated urgently. "Before someone sees you and figures out who I am."

"This is Boulder," she insisted. "You're being paranoid. You're safe here."

"No. I'm not. You're not, either, if you're around me. Go."

"I don't understand," she protested. "If all you're worried about is them finding you, why can't we meet in secret? There's so much we need to talk about, and you haven't even gotten to know your son. And—" She swallowed hard, pushing away her pride. "I've missed you, even if you haven't missed me."

"Lucy," he barked out her name. "That's not it at all. I don't want them to know I have a son at all. I don't want them to be able to use you against me. Understand?"

Though she didn't, not completely, there was no mistaking the apprehension in his voice. He really, truly believed the drug cartel had traveled all the way to Colorado on the hopes that he actually knew where to find their missing money.

Maybe he did have PTSD. Either way, she had no choice but to do as he said. But first, she had to tell him he had other allies.

"I'm going, I'm going." She turned around, wheeling a still dozing Eli away from his daddy. Though she thought she managed to keep her expression neutral, her mouth quivered. Sadly enough, she really wanted to cry.

She'd taken three steps before she felt compelled to look over her shoulder, to catch one last look of Tucker watching her leave. As she did, tires squealed. Someone shouted. Lucy spun around just in time to see a car careening up over the curb, coming into the pedestrian mall, and heading straight for her and Eli.

Eli! Her protective instinct kicked in and she leapt forward, shoving the baby stroller as hard as she could out of the way as she dove for a low stone wall and clump of bushes, hoping for some protection.

The car, low, black and foreign rushed past, then slammed on its brakes. Skidding sideways into a light pole, the BMW careened into a giant bronze statue of a buffalo with a clang.

Finally, the dust cleared and everything was still.

The driver didn't emerge from the vehicle and a crowd surrounded it, debating the best way to get him or her out.

Lucy rushed to reclaim her stroller. Baby Eli, now wide awake and upset, let out an ear-piercing wail. Just as she reached him, the BMW driver's side door opened on its own. A man got out, all dressed in black. He pushed through the crowd, heading toward her. It wasn't until he crouched and brought the pistol up to sight that Lucy realized he had a gun.

Suddenly, the situation Tucker had warned her about had become very, very real.

Acting on instinct, she ran, moving with Eli's stroller into the crowd of gawking bystanders, using them as a sort of impromptu shield.

"Come on." Tucker appeared beside her, unbuckling the baby from the restraining straps and scooping him up in his arms. "Leave the stroller. Let's go."

Without hesitation, she did as he said. Moving quickly, they wove through the gathering crowd, into a dark restaurant, blazing by a startled hostess.

"The back door is this way," Tucker said, brushing past the waitress's startled attempt to block them. They hurried through the kitchen, ignoring the busy cook and his helper, pushed open the back door, and came out into an alley behind the building.

"We've got to keep moving," he said.

"Where's your car?" she gasped, trying to catch her breath. Miraculously, all the activity had surprised Eli into silence.

"I don't have one." Tucker glanced around. "The DEA promised to bring me one, but they haven't yet. So, I'm going to have to steal one."

"I don't think that's a—" she began, but he wasn't

listening. He'd found a battered Toyota Corolla with the windows down.

"I can hotwire this. No enclosed dash," he said, already leaning in and hard at work. "Get in before the shooter figures out where we are."

Speechless, she climbed in. "We don't have a car seat," she said, aware her concern was foolish in light of the more pressing danger of some madman shooting at her.

The car started with a tinny little cough. "It can't be helped. Get in the back and lie down."

As soon as she had, Tucker put the Corolla in gear and drove away.

Once they'd exited the Pearl Street area, she poked her head up. "Where are we going? My house is that way."

The glance he shot her was both angry and amused. "You can't go back there. Now that they know you mean something to me, it isn't safe there."

She fought back panic. "You were serious."

"Of course I was." He shot her a look, probably amused, though she couldn't tell because of his dark sunglasses. "What did you think?"

"I don't know," she admitted. "I thought maybe you had PTSD and were sort of…paranoid. Imagining people were after you and all that."

Chuckling, he nodded. "I probably do have a little bit of PTSD. I was told to see a therapist and will, when this is over. But I can assure you I'm not imagining this."

"Unfortunately, I believe you now." Glancing out the window, she saw they were now heading out of Boulder. "Since I can't go home, where are you taking me?"

"To the place where I'm staying. Once I'm sure no one is following, that is."

To his house. She closed her eyes, aware how upset Sean would be.

Eli woke and stretched. He made a snuffling sound, the first hint he always gave when he was hungry. Just hearing that made her milk come in.

"I'm going to feed him," she said, aware she was avoiding the issue, but preferring to concentrate on her son.

Tucker didn't respond. The vehicle picked up speed, the engine whining. From the sounds of things, they were on the Diagonal Highway.

Sated, Eli fell back asleep.

Adjusting her blouse, Lucy looked up to see Tucker watching her in the rearview mirror. She longed for one aching second for him to remove the sunglasses once more so she could see his eyes, then chided herself for her own foolishness.

Meanwhile, time for her to face the music.

"I need to call Sean," she said, digging in her backpack for her cell phone.

"No." Tucker's sharp reply startled her. "You can't."

"I can't?" she repeated. Really, at this point nothing should have surprised her. In the space of less than half an hour, she'd found Tucker, nearly been run over, shot at, and now was speeding away in a stolen car to Tucker's hiding place. Sean was so not going to like this.

"I have to let him know where I am." She kept her tone reasonable. "If Eli and I simply disappear, he'll be worried."

Jaw working, Tucker finally nodded. "Fine. But make it short and sweet. Just tell him you're safe. No mention of where we are or especially that you're with me. Understand?"

Great. He wanted her to lie to her fiancé? She started to protest, then realized he was right. "For Sean's own safety, I'm guessing?"

"Exactly."

Luckily, she got Sean's voice mail. She left a brief message, telling him something had come up and she'd had to leave town. She told him not to worry and that she and Eli were fine. Then, her stomach clenching, she ended the call.

"He's going to call back as soon as he gets that," she told Tucker. "And he's going to expect more details."

Glancing back at her, one corner of Tucker's mouth lifted in a smile. "Of course he will. And, since you can't give him any, if I were you, I wouldn't answer the phone. My advice would be to turn it off."

Torn, she thought about it for a moment. Already she felt incredibly guilty, as though she was doing something wrong or unfair to Sean by omitting certain details. She'd feel ten times worse if he called and she ignored him. Shakily, she hit the button to switch off her phone.

There. It was done. "I don't believe this," she said, more to herself than to Tucker. "How can this be happening? We're in Boulder, Colorado, for Pete's sake, not one of the Mexican border towns."

"The drug cartel thinks I have their money. Even if I was in Alaska, they'd come after me for ten million dollars."

She bit her lip. "Then we need to notify the police."

"They already know," Tucker said, his deep voice soothing. "Though not the police. Actually, I'm working with the DEA to catch these people."

This was news to her. "Seriously? Why didn't you tell me this earlier?" Part of her felt he should have told her this up front. Like before he'd disappeared.

The rest of her felt like a fool for thinking he would.

"I was told not to," he said simply. "But since you're now right in the middle of this, I don't really have a choice."

That rankled. She wished it didn't.

"How long before I can go home?" Before she even finished asking her question, she had a feeling she might not like the answer.

He spared her another glance, the sunglasses effectively hiding any emotion. "You can't go home until it's over, Lucy. You and Eli won't be safe until then."

She couldn't really argue with his logic, but still... "How long will that be?"

"I don't know. Could be days, could be weeks or even months."

Months. Dizzy, she closed her eyes. "Sean's not going to like that."

He lifted one shoulder in a half-assed shrug. "He'd like it even less if you were killed. I'll keep you safe, Lucy. You and my boy." He glanced at the baby. "First thing in the morning, we'll go and buy a car seat, all right?"

Still shell-shocked, she nodded. "We need to stop and get diapers. I only have two spare ones in my backpack."

"Do they sell them at convenience stores?" he asked.

"I don't know. I'm guessing they might. And Tucker, I don't have much cash," she told him. "And I'm assuming we can't use credit cards because they can be traced."

"Don't worry about it. I've got it covered."

He pulled into a gas station with a convenience store attached. "Wait here."

A moment later, he returned with a large box of diapers. "I wasn't sure what size, so I got the closest ones to his age. Will these work?"

Suddenly tongue-tied, she nodded. "Thanks."

When they pulled up in front of the small frame house and she followed him inside, her skin prickled. She was suddenly overwhelmingly conscious of the utter weirdness of the situation.

Once upon a time, this would have been her every dream. Tucker alive and she and him, alone together. With Eli, their son. Like a family…and not. Because actually, they weren't. Nor could they ever be. She needed to remember that.

Nervously licking her lips, she told herself she could do this. She had to. She must keep things impersonal, friendly, and take care not to let the boundaries slide. Because she was, after all, promised to another. And, she reminded herself, any feelings she might have had for Tucker had died a year ago, when she'd thought he had.

She belonged to Sean now. And, once this was over, she'd return to him and marry him. That was the way things had to be, the way she wanted them to be.

Chapter 7

Following Tucker inside the house, Lucy took a deep breath and tried to calm her racing pulse and school her expression into one of polite disinterest. She hoped she'd marginally succeeded, though she doubted it because normally she wasn't any good at playacting. Tucker knew this.

Though she tried to appear cool, calm and collected, inside, she felt like a bundle of nerves. Her skin felt tight and she was antsy and sort of shaky, and uncomfortable. She just wished she could return to her normal life. But ever since learning he wasn't dead, her normal life had felt like an ill-fitting pair of shoes.

Even occupying the same space made her realize that the push-pull of attraction that had always existed between her and Tucker still did. Then she thought of Sean and felt guilty, even though she'd done nothing wrong. Physically, that is.

What was wrong with her, that she could love two men at the same time?

Unlike her, Tucker seemed completely at ease. He smiled easily and she didn't seem to make him feel jumpy the way he did her. Perhaps her engagement to Sean hadn't bothered him as much as she'd thought. Maybe—and she found the idea surprisingly and completely unpalatable—he didn't mind because he'd never wanted to take their relationship to the next level.

Despite his promise that they'd talk about it when he'd returned from Mexico, now she couldn't help but wonder if he'd been stalling her because he'd planned to break up. Though she'd never been able to imagine a time when Tucker didn't love her, maybe for him the love had died.

Of course, that had to be it. Ignoring the sharp stab of completely unwarranted pain the thought brought, she knew she should be rejoicing. All along, she'd been worrying about hurting him for no reason.

She should have felt relieved. Instead, she felt… confused and hurt. Damn him. When he'd "died," he'd left too much unresolved.

But what did any of that matter now? A year had passed and there was a lot of water under the bridge. She'd moved on, taking her life in a completely different direction.

Yet—to coin an absurdly overused phrase—maybe she needed closure. Perhaps that was why she'd been given this chance, why they'd been thrown together in such a crazy way. For closure. Once she'd obtained that, she could go forth and live her life with Sean with a clear conscience and unburdened heart.

Maybe she could vanquish that very small voice inside of her that said she didn't want to.

In order to even attempt such a thing, she knew she'd have to quash this still-insane attachment to him. Even now, promised to another man, she craved Tucker. It should have helped that he clearly didn't feel the same, but it didn't.

She could only hope time would heal this, too.

Because of the child they shared, she and Tucker would always have contact. She knew in time they'd have to become nothing but friends. For their son's sake. And for the sake of her own sanity.

She glanced at her baby. Their baby, tucked into the crook of his father's arm. Eli dozed, blissfully unaware of any changes to his life. Seeing the two of them, silhouetted in the late afternoon light streaming through the window, her heart felt so full she thought it would burst.

To distract herself, she glanced around. Tucker's little house, though sparsely decorated, was neat and clean and surprisingly cheerful. With Tucker and Eli there, the unfamiliar place felt more like home than her own house.

"I like it," she said, managing a wobbly smile.

"It came with a stocked refrigerator," he told her, smiling back. He'd finally removed his sunglasses and his beautiful blue eyes reflected nothing but friendly concern.

As they should, she reminded herself. As they should.

"It's a two bedroom." Leading her down the hall, he showed her where she'd be sleeping. Again, she was pleasantly surprised. Decorated in pale yellows and greens, the extra bedroom even had a bed, but no crib for Eli.

"I'm not comfortable letting him sleep in the bed with me," she said.

"Don't worry," he said, transferring the dozing baby gently back to her before crossing to the main dresser and pulling out a large, empty bottom drawer. "We can fix this up and make a perfect little place for him to sleep in."

Eyeing the drawer, which appeared to be solid and well-built, she supposed it would do. For one night only. She watched as he lined the drawer with soft towels, covering the sides and making a comfy little bed.

"How about that?" he asked.

Cuddling with her infant, she studied the impromptu sleeping area. "I don't know."

"It's well-padded," he said. "There's no way he can hurt himself."

Then, as she continued to hesitate, he reached out and squeezed her shoulder. The shock wave that went through her at his touch nearly sent her to her knees.

"You know I wouldn't suggest anything that could hurt him." His voice was gentle.

Finally, she nodded. "As long as it's solid, I guess it will be okay. But we'll need to add bassinet to our shopping list for tomorrow," she said, glad to have something else to focus on besides Tucker. "Along with sheets and a baby blanket. Oh, and you have no idea how many outfits a three-month-old baby goes through. And diapers. We'll need more of those."

She looked around for something to write with. "I need to make a list so we don't forget any—"

"Shhh," he said, surprising her by leaning in and kissing her hard on the mouth, midsentence, and effectively silencing her. "You're stressing yourself out."

Feeling that kiss all the way to her core, she froze, memories slamming into her. Tucker had always been more laid back than she, more impulsive and live-in-the-moment. He'd used to always tease her about her propensity for making lists. Her inclination to adhere to a strict routine had been something he'd been fond of disrupting.

She'd forgotten how much she'd missed Tucker's spontaneity. Sean was more like her.

Then, while she stood there gaping at him, he kissed her again. Every single resolution she had flew right out the window. It took every ounce of self-control she possessed to keep from wrapping her arms around him and taking that kiss to the next level.

"Calm down," he told her, still smiling. "Everything will be all right. We'll get it all handled. I promise. You and Eli are safe here."

Safe. The word sent a chill down her spine. Somehow, caught up in the thrill of being with Tucker, she'd managed to forget about the danger.

Tongue-tied, she looked down at her precious baby. Had she imagined the tenderness in Tucker's bright blue eyes? If not, that was most likely for his son, not her.

Which was as it should be, right? She wondered how many times she'd have to repeat that phrase to herself.

Being around him tied her stomach up in knots and turned her brain to mush. No matter how much she wanted to remain rational, common sense seemed to disappear the second she looked into his brilliant blue eyes.

As she looked up, Tucker leaned close, his voice

both husky and gentle. "Lucy, Lucy, Lucy. You haven't changed at all. What am I going to do with you?"

She opened her mouth to respond, but before she could, he leaned in and kissed her cheek again. The feather-light brush of his lips on her skin so shocked her, she couldn't move. Heck, she had to remind herself to breathe.

Okay, okay. She was sure he had only meant both kisses to be friendly, right?

Was she honestly disappointed? What was *wrong* with her?

"Please don't do that again," she said softly, her voice more shaky than she would have liked. "It isn't really appropriate under the circumstances." Now she sounded stuffy and stuck-up. "That didn't come out right."

"It's okay," he said, even though the expression in his eyes told her it was not. "I get it. You're engaged to another man. What happened to 'I'll love you forever, Tucker'? You said that to me once."

Pain shot through her. "I also thought it was time to take our relationship to the next level. You didn't. Tucker, I wasn't willing to be your girlfriend forever. I wasn't happy staying home while you traveled all over the world in search of a mythical coffee bean that probably doesn't even exist."

She took a deep breath, curious to see if he would interrupt her. When he didn't, she continued. "I wanted a family, a husband. Even if you hadn't 'died' in that plane crash, we would have probably gone our separate ways."

Eyes narrowed, he stared at her. "You really believe that?"

Sadly, she nodded. "I'd already decided. If you came back from Mexico and you weren't willing to commit, I was going to ask you to move out." Just saying this out loud for the first time made her stomach hurt.

Slowly, he shook his head, as though he could shake off her words. "What about Eli? How can you say such a thing when you were pregnant with my son?"

"First off, I didn't know that when I reached that decision. And second…"

"Second what?" he prompted.

"Second, I would never use our child to tie you to me." Straightening her shoulders, she lifted her chin. "Love that isn't given freely is no kind of love at all."

His rugged features had become an emotionless mask. "And now? I'm guessing you'd love to be able to get rid of me again."

"Don't be ridiculous. I love you—like a friend—and am relieved and overjoyed that you're okay. But, if I had a choice, I'd really like to go home."

"I can imagine." The starkness of his gaze never changed. "And I'm sorry that you can't. But I promise you that I'll make this as bearable as possible."

Bearable. If he only knew. Less than half a day alone with him and she already ached to touch him, to kiss him.

Searching for something to distract her from her decidedly wrong thoughts, she remembered the Toyota they'd hotwired in Boulder. "What are you going to do about the stolen car?"

"Good change of subject." He snapped his fingers. "Thanks for reminding me. I need to get rid of it. After we go on our shopping trip tomorrow."

"What if it's been reported stolen and the police notice it here?" She couldn't help but worry.

"Worrywart." Obviously he remembered this, too.

"For tonight, it should be fine parked in the drive behind the house. I don't think they'll see it."

Again silence fell. Once, quiet between them had been companionable. Now, it felt merely awkward, making her want to fidget.

"So," she asked brightly. "How about showing me the rest of your house?"

"It's not really mine." With a shrug, he moved toward the hallway. "And I'm only living here temporarily, until the DEA catches the bad guys."

"Yeah, about that." Following him, she noted the walls had been freshly painted and the wood-laminate floors appeared brand-new. "I have some questions about the whole DEA thing."

Pausing, he turned and she nearly ran into him in the narrow hallway.

"Right now?" he asked, his voice husky and low and dangerous, somehow. Or maybe it was her.

Struck dumb, she nodded.

"I'll give you the short version. The DEA has someone undercover in the cartel. That's how I was rescued. And because the bad guys think I stole their ten million dollars, the DEA asked if I'd let them use me as bait. They think I can lure the cartel's big boss out of Mexico and here. When he makes a move to grab me, they'll catch him."

"Sounds risky."

He shrugged. "Everything has some risk. I'd prefer to do it this way. I don't want to spend the rest of my life looking over my shoulder."

"I can understand that." Fighting against the urge to back up and put more than a few feet between them, she tilted her chin and looked up, studying him. "What about you? Do you think it's a good plan?"

"The truth?" At her nod, he continued. "No. It might work for them, but you know me. I'm not the type to sit around and do nothing."

And that was just it, exactly. She did know him. One year of him being gone didn't sweep all that away. She knew him better than anyone, better than she knew herself, sometimes.

"Do you have a better idea?"

His expression went cold, became shuttered. "I don't know," he murmured. "Do you still want to see the rest of the house?"

To find her voice, she had to clear her throat. "Sure."

"Then follow me."

After he finished giving her the grand tour, he led her back into the kitchen. The small room had white cabinets, green countertops and a beige, ceramic tile floor. The walls had been painted a reddish-orange. Surprisingly, the overall effect was cheery and homey. Just like the rest of the house.

"I like the colors here," she murmured. "And this house, it has a good vibe."

"I felt that, too. It's nothing fancy, but it's a solid little house."

Smiling up at him, she let herself momentarily bask in the warmth of his companionship. Momentarily.

"Are you hungry?" he asked, still smiling, meeting her gaze directly. The startling blue of his eyes still hit her like a punch in the stomach.

Hungry? She had to think about his question. She hadn't eaten since breakfast. "I think I am," she told him. "Yes. You said there's food here, right?"

"Yes." He gave her a sheepish smile. "There are dishes, glasses and silverware, too. I've got just about everything I need. Would you like me to make some spaghetti?"

Before his disappearance, when they'd lived together, they'd taken turns preparing meals. Tucker had been a fantastic cook. She'd relished the nights when it was his turn to make dinner. No doubt he remembered this.

And to think she'd believed she'd never get the chance to taste his cooking again.

"Spaghetti sounds great." Though she tried to curb her enthusiasm, she knew she was only marginally successful.

Tucker's grin widened, telling her he knew. "Spaghetti it is. Let me call my contact at the DEA first." Then he dialed a number, listened, then left a message. "He'll be calling me back," he said. "I'll get busy."

She fed Eli again while Tucker cooked. Walking around the small living room burping their baby, she listened to the domestic sounds coming from the kitchen. Pots clanging, Tucker humming and pretty soon the most delectable smells filled the air.

Tucker's Italian food was to die for. Her mouth watered just thinking about it.

"Do you want garlic bread, too?" he asked, coming around the corner to the living room.

"Yes, please." Catching herself grinning, she felt absurdly guilty, as though she shouldn't take so much pleasure in his company. But she couldn't help it. This was Tucker. She'd known him nearly all her life.

Before anything else, they'd been friends. The trio of them, the three musketeers, Tucker, Sean and her. Before he'd become her lover, Tucker had been her friend. That wouldn't vanish just because she'd agreed to marry Sean, would it?

She didn't think so. She really, really hoped not. Little

Eli would do so much better if both his parents got along.

Since Eli had gone back to sleep and was dozing, she went into the bedroom and placed him in the dresser drawer. He didn't wake and she stood a moment, gazing at the beautiful baby she and Tucker had created. Their child. A symbol of the love they'd once felt for each other.

When her eyes began to mist up, she stood and left the bedroom, calling herself a sentimental fool. Wandering into the kitchen, she eyed Tucker's broad shoulders, watching as he stirred something on the stove, and inhaled appreciatively. "That smells heavenly."

He grinned at her, making her entire body tighten. "It's almost ready. Would you like to pour the wine?" He indicated an open bottle of Chianti on the counter next to two stemless wine glasses.

"Wow," she marveled. "That was here, too? They gave you wine?"

"Yep. A bottle of red and a bottle of white. Along with a six-pack of beer. Whoever stocked this house really did think of everything. If I ever find out their name, I'm going to thank them personally."

She'd forgotten how his husky voice turned her insides to mush. Once, she reminded herself. No longer. Flustered, she moved forward and poured wine into both glasses, filling them halfway before carrying them to the table.

Tucker got the bread from the oven, then ladled spaghetti onto two plates and covered it with sauce. Though the sauce wasn't homemade, he'd clearly added to it.

"They didn't give me much in the way of fresh produce," he told her, sounding apologetic. "But I was able to find a can of mushrooms, and some diced tomatoes. I fixed the jar of sauce up the best I could with what I had."

Suddenly, she realized she was starving. "Sounds good." As she spoke, her stomach growled loudly.

He laughed. After a moment, she did, too.

Pulling out the closest chair, she inhaled happily as he placed her full plate in front of her. He went back for the bread and finally sat down across from her.

"Dig in," he said.

Eyeing the fragrant Italian food before her and the casual attitude of the man across from her, she felt something click inside her. This, despite the unfamiliar surroundings, felt like home. That had to be good, right? Maybe she actually could allow herself to relax.

They ate in companionable silence. Eli remained asleep, so she was able to finish her meal, snagging the last piece of garlic bread and using it to mop up her sauce. Full, she felt infinitely more serene. Sitting back in her chair, she sipped the last of her wine and watched Tucker inhale the final bit of his food. He ate like he did everything else—with enthusiasm. Just remembering what else he did with gusto made her entire body flush hot.

No. She wouldn't go there. Not now, not anymore.

He pushed back his empty plate, drained the last drop of his wine, and then looked at her, his blue eyes dark. "Did you like it?"

"Very much. Thank you. That was wonderful," she told him softly. For a split second their gazes locked and held. She broke the spell by jumping up and gathering the plates and utensils. It would be better, much better if she kept busy. "Since you cooked, I'll do the dishes."

"Not necessary," he started to protest, but it was only

halfhearted, as she'd known it would be. One cooked, the other picked up. After all, she and Tucker had lived together for over a year before his disappearance.

As she carried the plates to the sink, to her surprise, he went to the stove and began transferring the leftover pasta and sauce to a large bowl. "We can eat this again tomorrow."

Impressed, she nodded. "Works for me."

His smile broadened. "You know how just about everything is better the second time around."

Whether he'd meant that as an innuendo or not, heat flashed through her. Aware her face had probably turned beet red, she pretended not to get it and didn't answer, just turned back to the sink and continued rinsing off the plates and stacking them in the dishwasher.

Behind her, she was über-conscious of him as he stowed the leftovers in the fridge and wiped down the counter.

When she'd finished, she turned to find Tucker leaning against the counter, arms folded, watching her. She battled back a sudden, absurd shyness and tilted her head as she stared him down.

"What now?" she asked.

He glanced at his watch. "Well, we can either watch television or play Scrabble."

Zing. Another shared memory. Back before, they'd loved to play a rousing game of Scrabble on a Sunday afternoon. Though Tucker, with his propensity for making multiple words, usually scored higher than Lucy, she'd always had hopes of beating him.

"You have a Scrabble game here?"

"Yep. I was surprised when I found it in the front entry closet. Would you like to play?"

She couldn't resist. And worse, he knew it. Actually,

she realized she didn't care. "Scrabble," she said. Of course. He had to know she couldn't pass that up.

Expression impassive, he got out the board and set it up on the kitchen table, frowning as he worked. She let herself watch him, still standing back, feeling awkward and eager at the same time.

This entire situation seemed so surreal.

He glanced up at her and smiled again. "Would you like a beer or another glass of wine?"

Trying to pretend she hadn't felt his smile like a punch in the gut, she nodded. "Wine sounds great."

"I'll pour," they both said at the same time, both reaching for the bottle. As they collided, they both froze, staring at each other.

In his eyes, she saw warmth and some other, darker emotion that her mind shied away from recognizing. She lifted her chin. In hers, he no doubt saw her competitive spirit battling for domination.

"Are you ready?" His voice contained a challenge.

"I am."

They settled down to play. Though still acutely aware of him, she was glad to be able to focus on the game.

In the end, when all the tiles had been used, he had the most points. As always.

Tallying up the score, he put the pencil down and grinned at her. "Sorry, I'm still the unofficial Scrabble champion. But it was close."

She knew it wasn't. But his carefree grin so captivated her, she couldn't concentrate enough to protest.

Flustered again—really, she needed to get a grip on this—she jumped up and began gathering up the game pieces. The faux domestication of the scene brought back both memories and desires. She'd do best if she extricated herself from the room. But it was only eight o'clock. Far too early to go to bed.

Still, she could go check on Eli. Stammering out just that, she hurried out of the room.

Watching her go, Tucker could tell she was nervous. As far as she was concerned, the only good thing about this entire situation was that at least now he could get to know his own son.

For him, there was more. Not only was he allowed the joy of being with his own flesh and blood, but he got to spend time with her. Lucy, the love of his life.

For the first time in a long time, he could see a silver lining. Though he would have preferred for things not to have happened this way—the last thing he wanted was for Lucy and Eli to be in even the slightest bit of danger—he couldn't help but feel that this might be his lone chance to get Lucy back. Though Sean had gotten her to agree to marry him, Tucker knew she didn't truly love the other man. Not the way she'd loved him. Still did, he was willing to bet. He'd always been a gambling man. He'd risk it all—he had nothing to lose, anyway.

Lucy loved him. She had to. Otherwise, he might as well have died there in Mexico.

Either way, he planned to put it to the test. After all, if she really loved Sean, she'd have no trouble resisting Tucker's advances. And if she didn't love Sean, she had no business marrying him. He had to believe even Sean would have agreed with that.

Leaning back in his chair, he waited for Lucy to return. They'd been happy together, once. Memories of the life they'd once shared wouldn't be so easily erased.

His cell phone rang. Glancing at it, he saw it was Finn. Crap, he'd managed to conveniently forget about the DEA agent. It took a few seconds to bring him up to speed on what had happened.

Finn wasn't happy that Tucker had gone into Boulder and nearly gotten killed. He was even less happy to hear about Lucy and Eli, more so because he'd heard about it from another agent rather than Tucker.

"What was I supposed to do?" Tucker growled. "There's no way I could leave her at their mercy once they'd seen her."

"You were supposed to stay out of Boulder," Finn admonished. "None of this would have happened if you did as you were told."

Tucker cursed. "That's it. I've had enough. You seriously can't expect me to sit around in the tiny little house and act like bait. I've got to be proactive in this thing. And if that involves going to Boulder, then I'm going to Boulder."

"Yeah, look how well that worked out for you," Finn responded. "Come on. You can't bring a woman and an infant into this mess."

"You know what? You're absolutely right. You need to send someone to come get them and take them somewhere safe."

"That's the first rational thing you've said." Finn actually sounded relieved. "I'll send a team of agents first thing in the morning. We'll put her in a safe house until this thing is over."

Tucker's stomach dropped. He didn't know what he'd expected, but he hadn't thought Finn would actually do anything. So far the DEA agent had been sort of a hands-off kind of guy.

"Seriously?" he asked. "I'm actually not sure that's such a good idea."

"Why? You ought to rejoice. Once we remove them, you've got one less problem on your hands."

"One less problem?" Tucker repeated, actually regretting that he'd said anything. But then again…while he wanted to spend time with Lucy and Eli, their safety was more important.

"So I take it I shouldn't go through the hassle of buying a crib and sheets and all the stuff she wants me to buy?" Oddly enough, he felt kind of disappointed. He'd actually been looking forward to purchasing things for his son.

Finn laughed. "Go ahead. That way, the safe house we're sending her to will have everything she'll need."

"Sounds good." In fact, the whole situation sounded anything but. Tucker wanted to keep Lucy around, to give him time to get to know her again, win her over.

But he couldn't sacrifice her and the baby's safety for his own desires. "It'll be better all around if you take them away," he said. "I'm all for it."

A strangled sound behind him made him turn. Lucy stood in the doorway, one hand over her mouth, her beautiful eyes wide and shocked. Crap.

"Let me call you back." Without waiting for a response, he closed the phone. Lucy had taken off, heading toward the guest bedroom. "Lucy, wait."

As he rounded the corner after her, the front window exploded.

Chapter 8

The blast knocked Tucker to the floor. As he got up, he looked around frantically for Lucy. Having made it farther down the hall, she looked dazed, climbing slowly to her feet. She appeared unhurt. In the living room behind them, a fire raged, sending thick, black smoke ahead of it, toward them. From the age of the wooden house, he judged they had a matter of seconds to get out before the entire thing was engulfed in flames.

Lucy ran for Eli. Tucker sprinted after her. Once in the bedroom, he closed the door to provide a barrier against the smoke while she scooped up a wide awake baby. Panting, she turned to face him. "We've got to get out, but whoever did this is probably out front. Where do we go?"

"The way to the front door is blocked by fire, anyway," he told her, keeping his voice level. "Same with the back. We're going to have to get out this window."

Coughing as the acrid smoke began to fill the hallway and seep under the closed door, she nodded.

"We've got to watch out for the cartel's guys, okay?" He cautioned her as he unlocked and forced the large window open. Leaning outside, he checked both directions. "I don't see anyone. Come on. Hand me Eli."

As she glanced up at him, he felt gratified by the absolute trust he saw in her eyes. "I'll hold him while you climb out. Once you're outside, I'll pass him to you and I'll do the same."

Without hesitation, she did as he said, climbing over the sill and dropping the few feet to the ground, before reaching up so he could hand her Eli.

This done, he climbed out himself. Once they were all together, they glanced in both directions.

"It still looks clear," he whispered as sirens sounded in the distance. "If they're still here, they're in the front."

"What about the DEA?" she whispered back. "I thought they were supposed to be guarding you?"

"I did, too." Again he looked over his shoulder. "I'll check in with Finn later. Right now, we've got to get out of here."

Shepherding her in front of him, he hurried them over toward the small, wooden storage shed. Crossing behind that, they hugged the back of it, keeping to the grassy side yard opposite the garage and as far from the front of the house as they could get while staying in the yard.

"Just as a precaution," he told her, heart pumping. "Though I wish to hell the DEA had let me have a gun. I need something to protect us with."

"Well, since you don't have one, what now?" she

asked, still calm and rational, which he appreciated. The situation would be ten times worse if Lucy panicked. Maybe she understood how precarious their situation was. After all, she had their baby to keep safe.

As did he. And he would, no matter what.

"We've got to get out of here before the fire department arrives. Let's try to make it to the car, assuming it's still in one piece."

"Do you think they're still here?" Glancing back at the house, she trembled, the first sign she'd given since the explosion to show how this was affecting her.

"Who knows? I'm guessing they were instructed to scare us rather than kill us. Otherwise, they'd have rushed inside while we were still stunned and finished us off. So they're probably gone."

"Good." She took a deep breath. "I know we've got to get out of here, but why don't you want to wait for the fire department?" she asked, though she followed him as he moved cautiously around the back of the house. "I'm sure they could help us."

"They'll have a lot of questions which we aren't going to be able to answer. This isn't a normal fire," he told her. "Or a rational situation. Can you imagine their reaction if we start babbling about a drug cartel? They'll think we're crazy. No, we've got to get out of here before they arrive."

Motioning at her to hand him Eli, he pointed. "Are you ready?" At her nod, he dashed from the back of the storage shed to the back of the garage, carrying the baby, who'd remained amazingly silent. Lucy easily kept pace with him.

Moving around the side of the building, they reached the car without incident, which appeared undisturbed.

"I think they're gone." Opening the back door, he

motioned to her. "Get in and lie on the floor with Eli. Just in case." He didn't tell her he was worried they'd be shot at or followed. If that happened, he didn't want to take a chance of them seeing her and Eli.

Blessedly, she immediately did as he instructed. Backing the car out into the alley, he floored it and they careened away. No shots, no other car shooting out from a side street to follow them. He breathed a sigh of relief. In the distance, they could hear the loud wail of the fire-truck sirens as they drew closer.

"Are the people who did this gone for sure?" Lucy asked.

He took a deep breath, glad his pulse rate could slow somewhat. "It appears so, but stay down for a bit longer, just in case."

They made it back to the Diagonal Highway without incident. Once they'd gone a good distance away—with Tucker constantly checking to make sure they weren't being followed—he pulled the car into a fast-food restaurant at the south end of Main Street in Longmont and parked.

"I need to make a call," he told Lucy, punching in Finn's number in his cell from memory. "That DEA agent I told you about. I want to know what went wrong. He's supposed to have had men watching the house to make sure nothing like this could happen."

But after three rings, the call went to voice mail. He didn't leave a message.

"That's odd," he said, almost to himself. "He always answers the phone."

"The DEA agent?"

"Yeah. His name is Finn. He's my contact in the DEA."

"And that's who you were talking to earlier, about getting rid of me?"

"Yes, but it wasn't—" he began.

"I heard you. I know exactly what you said. I wanted to talk to you about that," she interrupted. Then, as she smoothed her hair away from her face with a shaky hand, she sighed. "Though I'm not sure I want to now."

He had to admire her strength. While she still appeared slightly shell-shocked—and who could blame her—apparently she remembered the conversation she'd overheard right before the explosion, and wanted to address what she thought she'd heard.

"If you have a question, please ask," he finally said.

"What did your contact at the DEA want you to do with me?" she asked. "I mean, you said I couldn't go home, so…"

"He was going to have you and Eli taken to a safe house tomorrow." He kept his tone firm, knowing she wasn't going to like the rest of what he had to say. "And Lucy, he still is, if we can get in touch with him before then."

"Away from you?" Her voice trembled, causing something to ache inside his chest.

"Yes." Ignoring her hurt look, he continued. "You'd be safer with them, and that's what's important."

"But—"

"If you can't think of yourself, consider Eli. We have to do everything we can to take care of him. Our son needs to be protected at all cost."

Finally, she nodded. "I don't like it, but you're probably right." She sighed. "I'll still worry about you, though."

Taking a chance, he reached out and brushed the hair

away from her cheeks. "Don't worry about me, honey. I can take care of myself."

Starting the car, he pulled out back on to Main Street. They stopped at the large discount store, went inside and because the situation had become precarious without the safe house, he purchased a car seat, a bassinet, more diapers and about ten different little outfits for Eli. "Is that enough?" he asked.

She laughed. "For a couple of days. As long as we have access to a laundromat or something, we should be okay."

They also bought themselves several changes of clothing and a knapsack to carry everything in. Tucker again used his credit card, wincing at the charge. He was perilously close to reaching the prepaid limit.

Once outside, he removed the car seat from its box, followed the instructions and set it up in the backseat of the car. This time, when they pulled out of the parking lot, little Eli was properly secured.

He drove slowly north on Main Street, glad no one knew him in Longmont. Finally spotting a pay phone outside of the old Lamplight Motel, he pulled over.

"I need to make a phone call. Wait in the car," he told Lucy.

"Again?" Then, as he opened his door, she grabbed at his arm. "Where are you going?"

He pointed. "To use that phone."

"Why a pay phone?" she asked. "Why not use your cell?"

"Because I'm keeping the cell phone off due to the GPS. A cell is too easily traced when one has the right equipment."

Frowning, she nodded. "So that's why you had me turn mine off?"

"Partially." He allowed himself a small smile. "But also because I know Sean. He would have been calling you nonstop. Eventually, he would have guilted you into answering. You know it, too."

Coloring slightly, she stared at him before nodding and turning to check on Eli in the back, now securely buckled in his brand-new infant seat.

Tucker let his gaze roam over her while she was distracted. Every time he looked at her, he felt the attraction clench his gut. She'd been his and he'd lost her. Only he couldn't reconcile himself to that fact.

If he could, he'd prefer to keep her with him, where he could maybe have a chance to see if she truly loved Sean or if she still belonged to him. But he had to put her safety above his own desires. Her safety and that of his son.

So far, he was doing all right at keeping them safe. He couldn't detect anyone following them or, for that matter, that they were under DEA surveillance like they were supposed to be. He wondered what had happened there, how the cartel had managed to circumvent the men who were supposed to be on guard. He still found it odd he hadn't heard from Finn.

Right now, it appeared he was on his own. The attack and explosion had changed everything.

Once out of the car, Tucker glanced around, making one final check of the surrounding area before approaching the pay phone. He saw nothing out of the ordinary. Lifting the receiver, he deposited the necessary change and considered. He thought he should probably call the main office of the DEA, but he didn't have the number. And quite frankly, the thought of all the explaining he'd have to do to get a hold of the right person made him impatient.

Instead, he took a chance and called Sean. "We're in trouble," he began. "I need your help."

"Where the hell are you?" Sean practically snarled. "Is Lucy with you? Don't bother lying to me. I know she is."

"Yes." Tucker gave his friend a straight answer. "And she's all right. Eli's fine, too."

"Why the hell are you dragging Lucy and Eli into this?"

"I'm not." Using as little detail as possible, Tucker explained what had happened at Pearl Street Mall. "I had no choice but to take her with me."

"Whatever. Tell me where you are so I can come and get Lucy."

With an effort, Tucker kept a grip on his irritation. "Have you not heard a single word I've said? Lucy can't go back to Boulder. They would go after her."

"Why? She's my fiancée, not yours."

Taking a deep breath, Tucker closed his eyes and silently counted to three. "They don't care about any of that. And they know Eli is my son."

"How? Did you tell them?"

"For the love of—" Tucker exploded. "Will you stop thinking of yourself and think of Lucy and Eli? My house was blown up and if I try to call the police, they won't believe me." For some reason, he didn't want to tell Sean he was working with the DEA. "I don't know where else to turn."

"If they found you once, they can do it again." Sean persisted, his hard tone sounding ruthless. "Lucy would be safer with me. I can utilize the security firm we use for the company. They can protect her."

"No, they can't. These guys have no mercy. I can protect Lucy."

"No, you can't. At least call the FBI or the DEA or somebody. Have them put Lucy in a safe house or something."

Exasperated, Tucker clenched his jaw. "Look, I didn't call you to talk about Lucy. I called to get your help."

Silence while Sean digested this obviously unpleasant news.

"What do you want me to do?"

Now came the delicate part. To get Sean to help him without letting him know too much.

"You want me to get a hold of the Feds? Fine, you do it for me. Contact the FBI and the DEA. There's a guy who debriefed me at the Mexican border when I was rescued. His name is Finn Warshaw. See if you can get a hold of him. I kept his card and called and left a message, but he hasn't called back. If you can't reach him, try and find out what happened to him."

"That name sounds familiar." Sean went quiet again. "I know. I saw it on the news. Finn Warshaw is in critical condition after a shootout in Niwot, of all places. Two other officers were killed. They haven't caught the suspects yet."

Niwot. At his house. Damn.

"You said your house was blown up?" A second later, Sean reached the same conclusion. "That was your place? Where there was an explosion, a fire and a shootout?"

Tucker winced. "Yep." He decided he didn't need to reveal that it had been a DEA safe house, though he wasn't sure why. Like so many other times in his life, he followed his gut instinct and stayed silent. No way did he plan to tell Sean the truth—that he was working with the DEA to bring down the cartel top brass. "And now not only does the cartel have me on the run, but I can't reach the one person I knew at the DEA."

Hearing the words out loud made him wince. Without Finn and the DEA behind him, what was he supposed to do? Try and catch the bad guys on his own? And what about Lucy and Eli? He had to make sure they were safe. Questions, questions, questions.

"What do you want me to do?" Sean sounded resigned. A little surprised that the other man wasn't going to push his insistence that Lucy be returned to him, which Tucker himself would have done, by the way, Tucker had to think.

"Actually, nothing." The decision took a split second to reach. "You've answered my question about Finn. Obviously, I'm on my own now."

"No, you're not. You can still call them, just speak to someone else. Think of Lucy and Eli. Get them somewhere safe in case the cartel is successful at finding you."

Sean sounded so ominous that his words had the opposite effect of making Tucker feel optimistic. Why, he didn't know, but still he had to bite his cheek to keep from chuckling.

"I'll take care of her. And Sean, I am sorry," he said, even though he was anything but. If he had his way, he planned to keep Lucy forever.

"Let me talk to her," Sean said.

"She's, er, busy." Tucker didn't even bother to try and hide the fact that he was lying. "As a matter of fact, I'm going to let you go now," he said. "We'll be in touch."

"Tucker, wait—"

Feeling like a heel, Tucker hung up the phone. No matter what, he and Sean had been best buds. He hated that for him to be happy, Sean would have to get hurt. Or vice versa.

Making his way back to the car, he pondered how much to tell Lucy. He'd prefer to stick as close to the truth as possible.

"Did you get a hold of anybody?" she asked, as he slid into the driver's side and fastened his seat belt.

"Not at the DEA. It turns out there was no need. I called Sean first."

"Why?" She sounded so surprised that he had to smile.

"Because I needed his help to find out what happened to Finn." He relayed the information Sean had given him.

For a split second she simply stared up at him, expression horrified. He so badly wanted to kiss her open-with-shock mouth, that he caught himself leaning forward.

"Wait. You're telling me that the government agents that were supposed to protect you—us—were shot and injured?"

"Two were killed, actually. Finn's the only one still alive." He took a deep breath, knowing she wouldn't like what he had to say.

"So we're on our own?" she asked, giving him a perfect lead to give her the unpleasant news.

"About that. While I'm sure the DEA will step up their game, especially since they lost their own people, I need you to be safe. I can't look after myself as well if I'm worrying about you and our son."

Though she visibly softened at the word "our son," she didn't respond, simply waited.

So he continued. "I still want you to go to a safe house. As soon as I can get a hold of someone there,

I'm going to ask them to come and get you. I want you to let the DEA take care of you and Eli."

"Right. Because they're just so good at it?" Glaring at him, she crossed her arms. "Nope. I'm not going. I'm staying with you."

"For your own safety—" he began.

She gave an inelegant snort. "My safety? I trust you to protect us better than them. Look at what happened in your so-called safe house. They kept you real safe, didn't they?"

"Okay, I'll concede that point, but—"

"No buts. Don't even bother asking them to get me. Because I refuse to go."

Though he wasn't entirely sure this was a good move on her part, he couldn't deny the relief that flooded through him at her decision. In fact, he was so relieved he finally gave in to desire and leaned over and kissed her, hard on the lips.

She felt exactly as he'd remembered in a hundred midnight dreams. Soft and warm and so damn perfect he ached for more.

But she moved restlessly, as though about to protest, and he forced himself to stop.

"I don't know…" she murmured, biting her lip. "What about—"

Before she could say Sean's name, he cut her off. "Don't. Not now."

As he lifted his head, she stared at him, mouth partially open, and something flickered in her expressive eyes. It might have been need, or pain, but he chose to call it desire, and leaned in for another kiss.

Suddenly, they were wrapped around each other, in each other's arms. They fit together as though carved from the same bone, two halves coming to each other and making a whole. His tongue met hers, sparring as she returned his kiss. For a moment, he couldn't catch his breath. He felt like a starving man given a feast. Lucy. Lucy. Lucy.

He couldn't get enough of her. Inhaling her familiar strawberry scent, letting his fingers caress her silky skin, joy hit him. So much more than mere desire. He felt as if he'd finally come home. Where he belonged. With her.

"Lucy," he murmured, making her name into a prayer. He kissed her again, unable to help himself, and whispered wordless endearments. Though he knew adrenaline likely fueled her desire, he'd take what he could get.

Time and place ceased to matter. They were together again, craving each other, and need and desire and emotion tangled up in two bodies trying to become one.

They were, he thought in a single coherent moment, making out in the front seat of the car like a pair of horny teenagers who'd been kept apart too long.

He didn't care. This was something he'd dreamt of for an entire year. She was his and he belonged to her. To think anything else would be sheer madness.

Gliding his fingers over the perfect swell of her breasts, he reached up under her shirt and cupped them, her nipples hard and aroused. She moaned, pressing herself against his hand. Damn. He bit back his own cry, fighting his own arousal and the threat of lost control.

Which he would not allow. He wanted to savor this moment, revel in her. He'd been denied her for so long, he couldn't blow it now.

When he skimmed his hand down her side, to the

curve of her hip, she leaned into him, pressing her full breasts into his chest.

"It's been too long," she murmured against his mouth, her eyes closed as she caressed him fiercely, possessively. "I've missed you so much."

Her words, along with her touch, only served to inflame him even further. "Ah, Lucy." He wanted more. Much more. Right. Now.

Then suddenly, Lucy stiffened and pulled away. "Any moment now, the police are going to show up and tap on your window," she said breathlessly. "And since this is a stolen vehicle, it might be a good idea for us to get moving."

At first, his desire-fogged brain had difficulty comprehending her words. Then, as the meaning sunk in, he realized she was right.

Damn it. They needed to go somewhere else. His body throbbed, needing her, wanting her, craving her. They should go to a motel. They would have to anyway, or else sleep in the car. Which wouldn't be good for them or baby Eli, still sleeping in his newly purchased car seat in the back.

Adjusting his clothing, aware she could see the strength of his arousal, he pondered how to best broach the subject.

"How about we find a hotel room where we can stay. Maybe one of those extended-stay places," she said, effectively taking the pressure off him. "We've got to sleep someplace. Then we can see about ditching this car and finding us something else to drive—hopefully legally."

"Sounds good," he said, relieved and trying like hell not to picture all the things he wanted to do to her in a proper bed. Then, just as he successfully quashed the rather graphic images, she spoke again.

"And Tucker, make sure you get us a room with two beds."

"Let me turn my phone back on and see what I can do," he said. Digging it out of his pocket in his inflamed condition wasn't easy, but he did it, sucking in his breath sharply when he saw the Missed Call message with Finn's number on the screen.

Immediately, he pushed the Call Back button.

It rang twice, before someone answered with a garbled hello.

"Finn?" Tucker said, continuing without waiting for a reply. "Are you all right?"

"Listen carefully, you American idiot," a heavily accented voice said. "We will find you soon and then you will die."

Not Finn. Definitely not Finn. He must have dropped his phone when he'd gotten hurt. And now someone in the cartel had it and was using it to call Tucker. Worse, the voice didn't sound like Miguel Gonzalez. Which could mean nothing, or everything.

"I don't have your money," Tucker said. "And killing me isn't going to help you find it."

The other man cursed in Spanish, the angry tone virulent.

"I don't know why you think you can get away with stealing from us," he spat. "But we will find you and we will make you pay."

"For the last time, I don't have your money," Tucker told him. "I don't even know who has it, or where it is. You're wasting your time with me."

"That's not what you said before. You told Miguel

that you were willing to work a deal. There will be no deal! We won't pay for what is already ours."

With Finn out of commission and no idea if anyone else in the DEA was working this case, Tucker figured it would be best to try to come clean, though he wouldn't give away the undercover operation and endanger any agents still in the field.

"I lied," he said, well aware there was no way in hell they were going to believe him. "I don't have your money. I don't even have any idea where it might be."

But he was speaking to dead air. The other man had ended the call.

Immediately, Tucker switched his phone back off. "Hell."

"I take it that wasn't the DEA?" Lucy asked dryly.

"No. And that guy—whoever he was—wouldn't listen to reason."

"Did you really expect him to?" she asked. "From the sounds of it, these cartel people seem pretty determined to believe you have their money."

"I know. And I really don't understand why."

"Then maybe we need to think about this. Who else could have stolen their money?"

"I'm not sure. I'm completely unfamiliar with these drug cartels and how they operate."

"Well, maybe we need to try and find out. From the sound of things, that might be the only way out of this."

He stared at her, his heart swelling with love and pride. "You know, with the DEA so focused on setting up a sting to capture the leaders of the cartel, I never thought about finding the real thief. You might just have something there."

Caramel eyes shining, she smiled. "Thanks. The question is, how do we go about it?"

Chapter 9

Lucy felt, irrationally she knew, that if she were to let Tucker out of her sight, something horrible would happen. Whether to him or her, she didn't know or really care. There was no reason involved with this feeling, just an impending sense of doom that felt completely at odds with her normal sense of optimism.

So when they pulled up in front of the large, extended-stay motel, she insisted on going inside with him. With Eli in her arms, she watched while he procured them a room for a week, using his DEA-issued credit card. After all, he figured they were still monitoring his whereabouts.

Then, after checking out their room, which was basic, double bed, bland colors, worn shag carpeting, they lay side by side on the bed, intended only to rest for a few hours. Instead, when Lucy opened her eyes again, bright sunlight streamed through the grimy window. And the spot on the bed next to her where Tucker had been was empty, though she could hear the sound of the shower running.

Eli, also awake, smiled at her from his makeshift bed. Picking him up, she changed him and then nursed him while waiting for her turn in the bathroom.

When Tucker emerged, his hair damp and slightly wavy, the sight of him made her stomach clench. "Your turn," he said, smiling. "I'll watch Eli while you get ready."

Unable to find her voice, she simply nodded. She hurried through her shower, brushed her teeth and then lightly blow-dried her hair. Then, dressed and feeling a hundred times more awake, she opened the door to find Tucker cradling the baby, who'd fallen sound asleep. This time, she felt a hitch in her heart, as well.

"Let's grab a bite to eat," Tucker suggested, apparently oblivious to the perfect domestic picture he made. "It'll be another hour or so before the car dealers open."

Car dealers? That made perfect sense. They needed to ditch their stolen vehicle, but they'd need a replacement to drive.

After going through the drive-through at McDonald's restaurant down the street, they parked and devoured their breakfast sandwiches and steaming coffee. Then they drove back to the southeast side of Longmont. There, they ditched the car on a back street near the old turkey slaughterhouse. They made a small ceremony of it, only half joking, thanking the car for its service above and beyond the call of duty.

Tucker removed the car seat, which converted easily to an infant carrier. Once she had Eli buckled back in, Tucker took him from her and they walked, side by side like a real family, all the way back to Main Street.

Luckily, clouds had rolled in from the mountains and the temperature was bearable.

A few blocks north, they found a large used car dealership.

Together, they picked out the oldest, most battered car on the lot, a faded red Honda that had definitely seen better days.

The gum-chewing, balding salesman could barely tear his gaze away from the old *I Love Lucy* rerun on the television to inform them he wanted fifteen hundred.

Moving around to partially block his view of the flat screen, Tucker talked him down to twelve. Doing the math, he figured he had barely enough, so again, he paid with his credit card. Once the charge went through, the salesman handed over the title and the necessary paperwork they'd need to get the license plate at the local tax office.

Though she tried to appear cool, calm and collected the way Tucker appeared to be, she felt like a jittery bundle of nerves. She had to stop herself from constantly glancing out the window to make sure they weren't being followed. She supposed she'd feel slightly better once they were in the car, but these people were so ruthless they didn't seem to care that Eli was an innocent and shouldn't be targeted. She couldn't let anything happen to her son.

"Mission accomplished," Tucker told her, grinning as they walked out to take possession of their new ride.

She somehow managed to smile back, wondering why she felt way more alive in these moments with him than she'd felt in the entire year he'd been gone from her life. It crossed her mind to wonder what this said about her future with Sean, but she put that out of her mind as quickly as she could. No doubt it was merely adrenaline due to her heightened sense of danger.

It took a few minutes to get the car seat set up in the back and Eli buckled in. Then, Lucy climbed in the passenger side and Tucker started the engine.

"And we're off," Tucker said with a laugh.

"Thank goodness." Lucy found herself smiling back. "Though this has, without a doubt, been the weirdest few days of my entire life, I finally feel like this is the first time I can relax. Things sure have been crazy since I ran into you at the Pearl Street Mall."

He shot her another one of those half smiles that made her heart skip a beat. "Sorry about that. I was expressly told to stay out of Boulder."

She wasn't sorry, though she didn't voice the thought out loud. Instead, she asked a question. "Why were you there in the first place?"

"The cartel sent somebody to the BBB offices. I almost intercepted him once. The DEA had an agent shadowing me, too, I guess to make sure I didn't get hurt or captured. I wanted to try and talk to the guy in a public place. I was hoping to catch him by surprise. Though it was unlikely I'd get that lucky twice, I thought it was worth a shot."

Unsurprised, she looked at him. "Sean said the guy was with the Mexican Consulate. But he thought the same as you, that the cover story was a lie."

"Yeah." Drumming his fingers on the steering wheel, he seemed lost in thought. "I'd really like to know how I got involved in all this mess. One minute I'm a normal guy visiting Mexico to buy coffee beans, the next, I'm being held prisoner by a drug cartel and suspected of stealing ten million dollars. It doesn't make sense."

"And in the process, your life got ruined."

He turned and stared at her. "Yours did, too, Lucy Knowlton," he said softly. "And I dare you to deny it."

She had nothing to add to that, so she merely nodded.

After hitting the drive-thru of a fast food place to pick up some drinks, they headed back to their temporary abode. When they reached the motel, Tucker parked and she got Eli out of his car seat. This time she carried him and Tucker carried the tray with their drinks.

Her stomach growled loudly, making her smile.

But once they were inside, her nervousness came back full force. She didn't understand why she was so on edge—she believed she had enough self-control to resist Tucker. She had to, if she didn't want to get her heart broken again. Plus, she had Sean to consider. Her fiancé. She needed to remember that, especially if Tucker kissed her again.

She'd never been the kind of woman to cheat. She hadn't even been able to bring herself to be intimate with Sean yet. Even though she'd believed Tucker to be dead, each time Sean tried, she'd resisted. It felt too much like cheating.

Again, she had to wonder what that meant about her future.

To distract herself, she fed her son, overly conscious of Tucker's presence. He stood there, devilishly handsome, trying not to watch as their baby nursed. Then, once Eli had had his fill and fallen asleep, she buttoned up her shirt and looked up to find Tucker looking at her with so much longing in his gaze that she gasped, feeling like she'd been punched in the stomach.

Eli yawned and she gently placed him on the brand-new sheets in the bassinet.

Then, because Tucker seemed to be waiting expectantly and because she ached for his touch, she said the one thing that might have a chance of dousing the heat that was building up between them.

"I think I need to call Sean," she said quietly.

Her words had the expected effect. Tucker's expression shut down, the tenderness in his eyes turning to stone.

"Why now?" he asked, reminding her how well he knew her. "Are you having second thoughts?"

Because there'd always only been honesty between them, she gave him the truth. Even though she wasn't sure which situation he referred to. "Yes."

He nodded. "Take your time. Just remember, you don't have to do anything in a hurry."

Again, she couldn't tell if he meant with him or Sean, so she lowered her gaze in confusion.

Uncertain how to react, she went into the bathroom to freshen up. Once inside, she realized she wanted a long, hot shower, so, poking her head out into the other room, she asked Tucker if he would keep an eye on Eli.

Barely looking up from the television, he readily agreed.

Stepping into the shower, she stood under the hot water and let it wash away the last few days. She hated this. Indecision made her stomach ache. Maybe she needed to forget about both the insane need for Tucker and her obligation to Sean and focus on what was important—keeping Eli safe.

Easier said than done. Her thoughts kept returning to the man in the other room and the incredibly passionate kiss they'd shared. The moment they'd touched, it was like the past year had simply melted away.

Obviously, she still had feelings for him. She'd never been one to lie to herself, and the kind of love she felt for Tucker would not be easily discarded. Once, she'd known without a doubt that he was The One, her soul mate, the only man she'd ever love. In her heart of hearts, she knew twelve months hadn't changed that.

Could she keep those emotions at bay? Should she? She was engaged to another man. How did that factor in? If she still loved Tucker, then what about Sean? She loved him, too, of course. Just in a different way. Was that enough? Not for her. And she suspected not for him, either. He'd already made it clear that he didn't want to be second best.

Ah, so much turmoil. She thought of the year she'd spent on her own. She'd carried Eli to term while mourning Tucker. Sean had made sure she'd never been lonely. He'd been there whenever she'd needed him, but she'd managed to function well on her own, birthing her healthy baby with Sean as her coach.

After she'd come home from the hospital, she'd taken care of Eli completely by herself. Oh, Sean had popped in frequently and been her biggest supporter, but she'd been proud of how self-sufficient she was as a brand-new mother.

She'd honestly thought she'd spend the rest of her life single. After Tucker, she'd known she'd never want another man.

Through it all, Sean had made no secret of his feelings. He told her often he loved her and wanted her to share his life. At first, she hadn't been able to hide her surprise, as she'd always thought of him as a friend, nothing more.

She'd turned down his first marriage proposal and each subsequent one after that, always being careful to explain, even if it sounded like a clichéd line, that it wasn't him, it was her.

He'd vowed never to give up. And he hadn't. Instead,

he'd doggedly continued his pursuit. When he'd proposed for the third or fourth or fifth time a few days after the one-year anniversary of Tucker's so-called death, she'd actually hesitated before turning him down.

Taking advantage of the first crack in her armor ever, Sean had pressed his point, bringing flowers, a bottle of wine, even though she couldn't drink it since she was nursing, and pouring out his heart to her.

He said he'd always loved her, even though she'd had eyes for no one but Tucker. This made her sad. Because, while she loved him like a friend, she didn't feel the same way about him.

He wasn't Tucker. Plain and simple. Worse, she knew there'd never be another Tucker for her.

Wanting to be honest, she'd told Sean this. Though hurt had darkened his eyes, he told her he didn't care. He still wanted to marry her.

This surprised and humbled her. Suddenly, she saw her choice quite clearly. She could marry Sean, a man she'd known nearly all her life, or stay single, raising her son on her own.

Sean was a decent man, a good man who happened to love her. Accepting his proposal would make him happy. Watching him interact with her son, whom he so clearly loved, she made a decision. Eli would need a father, especially as he grew older. She would marry Sean.

Once she'd accepted his proposal, Sean had been ecstatic. He'd produced the ring—one he'd purchased before the first time he'd proposed, and joyfully placed it on her finger. Branding her as his.

If she'd felt pangs of unease, she'd buried them. She would do what was right for her son. But she'd soon begun to have the nightmares again. The worst part of the entire thing was that she suspected she was marrying Sean because he, too, had been close to Tucker.

She loved him like a friend. Eventually, she believed that would be enough.

And then…she'd answered her doorbell and everything changed.

Tucker, larger than life. One look from his sapphire eyes and she'd been lost.

Still was, as a matter of fact. She sighed, letting the hot water sluice down her body. Tucker was back. His kisses still seared her soul, but he didn't appear to have changed. She'd loved him so much before and his reluctance to commit had hurt so badly. She wasn't sure she could put herself through that again. Did she really want to let herself love him again, only to watch him vanish once more on his expeditions for days or weeks at a time?

Did she even have a choice?

Rinsing the shampoo out of her hair, she turned the water off and grabbed a towel. Best to keep her distance—at least emotionally—from Tucker while she figured out where her heart belonged.

Clean and feeling invigorated, now that she'd reached a decision, she put on some of her new clothes and emerged from the bathroom. She stopped dead at the sight of Tucker grinning at her from where he'd sprawled on the bed, waiting. Even in the dim lamplight, he looked so masculine and beautiful it made her heart ache.

"My turn," he said, jumping up and disappearing into the bathroom. A moment later, she heard the shower start.

Despite turning the TV on in an attempt to distract herself, she couldn't stop imagining Tucker, naked under the running water. Before his disappearance, she'd often slipped into the shower to make love with him. It had been one of her favorite things to do. Remembering this now aroused her more than she could believe.

She wondered if Tucker remembered, too, and if he did, if the memories would stir him as much as they did her.

The thought sent heat through her. Disgusted with herself and her train of thought, Lucy climbed up in the bed and closed her eyes, trying to sleep. But, even though her body was exhausted, all she could think about was Tucker and how badly she wanted him.

Over him? Apparently not.

"I'm not that kind of woman," she said out loud.

"What kind of woman do you mean?" Tucker asked, emerging from the bathroom in time to hear her.

Blushing, she sat up and lifted her chin as she decided to be honest. "The kind that sleeps with one man while engaged to another."

He stared at her, the silence making her want to squirm.

"But you were thinking about it?" he finally asked. "Sleeping with me, that is?"

She nodded.

"Well, that's progress, at least," he said, surprising her. "Because I've thought about that a hell of a lot."

"Don't—"

Ignoring her interruption, he continued on. "Now, though I hate to change such an interesting subject, are you hungry? For food, I mean. Do you want to go grab something to eat?"

Completely and thoroughly embarrassed, she actually had to think about whether or not she could eat. She'd been obsessing over her inappropriate desire to the exclusion of anything else.

"I think so," she finally answered, well aware her color was high. "What did you have in mind?"

"There are a bunch of fast-food places on Main, but I'd love to have a good steak. There's a Texas Land and Cattle. How about there? I can use up the remaining money on this prepaid credit card."

"Or I can use one of mine," she said. "But while that sounds fantastic, is it safe for us to eat out inside at a restaurant?"

He shrugged. "Should be. Right now, the cartel has no idea where I am. Niwot is halfway between Boulder and Longmont, so I could be in either city, not to mention Denver and all the suburbs. The odds of them running into us aren't very high."

He seemed so nonchalant. Then she remembered—the higher the stake, the more casual Tucker's demeanor. Which meant the situation was dangerous indeed. She suppressed a shiver. "How high?" she persisted. "I don't want to take any unnecessary risks with Eli."

"Next to zero." He met her gaze straight on. "I imagine the DEA will be all over that house in Niwot, especially since they lost men. The cartel will be laying low for a while."

Showing her fear wouldn't help. Resolutely she straightened her shoulders and subdued her terror.

"Then that sounds good." Forcing a smile, she knew she shouldn't have felt so depressed at his lighthearted tone. Obviously, despite the passionate kiss they'd shared, she didn't affect Tucker nearly as strongly as he did her.

Once again, just like before, even if they were to pursue the attraction between them, their relationship would be uneven. Back then, she'd been aware that she'd loved him more than he loved her. Apparently, that went the same way for desire.

A good thing, she told herself. Once again proof that she'd made the right choice by choosing Sean.

Tucker thought he'd explode from trying to hide his desire. The second he'd stepped into the shower, vivid memories of a naked Lucy joining him had assaulted him. The things they'd used to do with the water raining down on them! He'd been so aroused by the time he was done washing himself, that he'd had to turn the water to cold to reduce the size of his massive arousal.

Worse, she had no idea what she did to him. Or, he reflected grimly, maybe that was all for the best. As long as he could appear indifferent to her charm, he held the upper hand.

Buckling a drowsy Eli into his infant carrier/car seat, Tucker glanced up to catch her watching him. He couldn't read the expression in her long-lashed gaze.

"What's wrong?" he asked gently.

"I just wish everything could be normal." She swallowed hard and he realized she struggled not to cry. "Like it was before you went to Mexico in the first place."

"Me, too, Lucy," he said. "Me, too."

They arrived at the restaurant and parked. Once they'd gotten Eli out and removed his car seat to use as a carrier, he insisted on being the one to carry him. How right the three of them together like a family felt never ceased to amaze him. And he wanted this—forever—with a hunger that should have surprised him, but didn't.

After all, Lucy didn't know that one of the things

he'd lost when he'd been captured had been a beautiful solitaire diamond ring. When he returned from the coffee-buying expedition to Mexico, he'd planned to ask her to marry him.

Full, Lucy sat back in her chair and sighed. The meal had been wonderful, reminding her of old times. They'd managed to forget the dangers of their current situation, if only for a little while. And being out in public had helped her regain control of her wayward thoughts and unreasonable desire.

Ordering fried pickles as an appetizer, they'd had steaks and even shared a dessert. Little Eli had slept through the entire meal, allowing Lucy time to eat and relax. She hadn't felt so much like a family since Tucker had disappeared.

And she was happier than she'd been since he'd disappeared.

So what did that make her? Flighty? A woman who turned from one man to the other, then back again? Was she one of those women who needed a man to feel complete? She didn't like either of these descriptions.

She'd been too hasty in accepting Sean's proposal. Regardless of what happened with Tucker, she needed to end things with Sean at the earliest opportunity.

By the time they got back to the hotel, darkness had fallen. They'd taken turns changing in the bathroom, Lucy first.

Once she'd closed the door behind her, she turned on the water full blast, then pressed the on button on her cell phone. Pulling up her contacts, she called Sean.

He answered on the second ring. "Where the hell are you?"

"I'm safe," she said, swallowing hard. "Sean, we need to talk."

"Don't do this," he said, immediately intuiting what she was about to say.

"I have to. Sean, I can't marry you."

He cursed. "You're back together with him."

"No. No, I'm not." Her chest hurt. "Not yet. Maybe not ever. I'm not sure I can go through all that again. But it would be wrong to be engaged to you, knowing…" She couldn't finish, her eyes filling with sudden tears.

"I'm second best," he finished for her, his voice furious and raw. "Once again, that bastard wins."

She felt as though by hurting him, she was also ripping her own heart out of her chest. "I'm sorry," she whispered. "He doesn't even know I'm calling you. I didn't want to hurt you."

"What now, Lucy?" He practically snarled the words. "What's going to happen now?"

Her voice sounded small. "I was hoping we could still be friends."

"Friends?" He laughed, a bitter sound. "Seriously, Lucy? You agree to marry me, and then cheat on me two weeks later? Do you really think calling me up and telling me that I'm once again second best would make me want to be your friend?"

"I haven't cheated on you."

Instead of responding, he ended the call.

Hating that she'd hurt him and hurting herself, Lucy turned her phone off and stuck it back in the pocket of her jeans, along with her engagement ring. She'd return that to Sean as soon as she could.

Then she got undressed and put on an oversize T-shirt and shorts. She splashed cold water on her face and blotted it dry. Taking a deep breath, she composed herself and exited the bathroom.

Keeping her head down to avoid meeting Tucker's gaze, she hurried to her bed. Climbing into it, she pulled the sheet up to her chin and focused on the TV.

"My turn," Tucker said cheerfully, shooting her a curious look before disappearing into the bathroom.

The instant the door closed behind him, Lucy pulled out her phone again, trying to decide whether or not to call Sean again and try to explain. Assuming he would even talk to her. She couldn't really blame him for his anger.

Finally deciding that he needed time to calm down, she placed the phone on her nightstand and focused on the television. If she could somehow fall asleep before Tucker emerged, it would be for the best.

But, with her emotions running high and her stomach churning, she couldn't sleep. Instead, she tried to concentrate on watching the television. The crime melodrama was intense and easy to follow and she was glad of the distraction.

A few minutes later, when Tucker emerged wearing a T-shirt and boxers, her mouth went dry and all rational thought fled.

Damn. Gazing up through her lashes, she let her eyes roam over him. Tucker. He looked the same—broad shoulders, narrow waist, muscular arms—yet different. There were sharp edges to him now, angles and shadows that hadn't been there before.

No matter what he looked like, she knew he'd always be the ultimate male in her eyes.

She'd thought she could erase him from her memory. Now, she realized no matter how many years passed or how great the distance between them, no other man would ever measure up. And, while she didn't know whether she and Tucker would be able to get back together again, she knew she'd always love him.

She'd done the right thing, breaking up with Sean. No matter how much she might have hurt him now, she knew she'd rectified the mistake she'd made in accepting his marriage proposal while still in love with another man. In time, she knew Sean would see that, too.

So where did that leave her? Aching and feeling foolish.

The television show she'd been watching ended and the early news came on. They both pretended an avid interest as the newscaster announced the latest baseball scores.

Next, they showed Tucker's burned-out house in Niwot. The ongoing investigation, according to the newscaster, had focused on a local gang.

"Local gang?" Lucy asked, incredulous. "Are they for real?"

"I'm sure that's the story the DEA is putting out there."

The short segment ended and a commercial came on.

"I'll try to contact the DEA again first thing in the morning," Tucker said.

"No safe house," she told him firmly.

"We'll see," he answered. "I want to do what's best for you and Eli."

Finally, the news came to an end and Tucker turned the TV off.

"Good night, Lucy." His deep voice made her shiver.

Calling herself all kinds of a fool, it took a moment before she could coherently respond. "Good night."

She switched off her bedside lamp first and a moment later Tucker did the same. Rolling on her side, she told herself to get some sleep.

A moment later, she turned to the other side, unable to get comfortable. Knowing Tucker slept less than ten feet away from her did strange things to her equilibrium.

To distract herself, she checked on Eli, slumbering soundly in his portable bassinet. As soon as she was able to determine that her baby was fine, she fluffed up her pillow and tried once more to go to sleep. The bedside digital clock showed ten minutes had passed. Then twelve. Fifteen. Twenty-one.

Tucker. She wanted to go to him, especially if he really meant to send her away tomorrow. Too much time had passed since she'd been able to wrap herself around him and she didn't know how long they'd be apart this time.

At the very least, she wanted him to hold her.

From that single thought, her imagination took flight. They'd always fit well together, as though she were made for him. She ached to feel him inside her again.

Damn, she was in trouble.

Lying in the dark with him, side by side in separate beds, while their child slept nearby, her desire intensified, becoming so strong she knew she wouldn't sleep. Her entire body burned with need.

In the bed next to her, she judged from Tucker's ragged breathing that he had the same problem. "Tucker?" she said, then mentally kicked herself for speaking. "Are you—?"

"Yes, I'm thinking about you," he said, his voice harsh. "Fantasizing about you. And yes, Lucy, I want you. More than you could ever believe."

She gasped as need and desire blossomed through

her. So much for careful resolutions and planning. She could no more resist this man than she could stop breathing.

If that made her a fool, then so be it.

Chapter 10

Gathering up all of her nerve, she threw back the covers, got out of bed and crossed the space dividing them. When she reached his bed, she took a deep breath, wondering if she could physically take such a huge leap of faith.

An entire year had passed. Twelve months of mourning Tucker, missing Tucker. She hadn't made love to anyone in all that time, including Sean. She simply hadn't been ready and he'd claimed he understood. Sometimes she'd wondered if her desire had died with Tucker.

Now, he'd returned and suddenly, every bit of her had come alive. How could she not make love with him now that they were together again?

Lifting the covers, she froze as he used his hand to grab her arm, effectively keeping her immobile.

"What about Sean?" he rasped.

She swallowed, almost afraid to tell him the truth, though she had no reason not to. "Sean and I are no longer engaged. I called him a little while ago and ended it."

Still he gripped her tight. "Because?"

"He's a good man, Tucker," she said.

"I never said he wasn't. Why did you break off your engagement?"

Oh, no, she wasn't going there. "I refuse to cheat on him."

"That's a given." He massaged her arm with his thumb, relaxing his grip slightly. "You're not the cheating type."

"No," she said shortly. "I'm not."

"But Lucy, there has to be more. Obviously, if you want to be with me, you didn't love Sean."

Then, she understood. Tucker wasn't the cheating type, either. He wanted to make certain that she wasn't acting on impulse, going with the spur of the moment. He needed to know for sure that she didn't truthfully belong with Sean.

"I never should have accepted his proposal," she said truthfully. "It would have been better all the way around if we'd stayed friends. I don't love Sean," she managed softly. "Not the way I should to have considered marrying him."

He went silent for so long she began to wonder if he'd actually dozed off. Except he still held tight to her arm.

Then she realized he was waiting for her to say something more. Something she wasn't willing at this moment to say. If he wanted a declaration of love, he wasn't going to get it. Her private heart would remain exactly that—private.

Finally, he spoke. "Thank you, Lucy."

The calm certainty in his voice pissed her off. "You know what, I've changed my mind. Let me go." She tried unsuccessfully to shake off his grip. "I need to get some sleep."

Instead, he yanked her, pulling her on top of him. She gasped sharply as their bodies collided. "Tucker…"

"Shhhh," he murmured, nuzzling her neck. "It'll be all right again."

What little resistance she'd managed to muster was rapidly fading. He smelled marvelous, like man and soap and toothpaste. All she could hear was her fast breathing and the equally rapid beat of her heart.

Turning her head, she let his mouth find hers. Instant electricity blossomed, blowing away any lingering doubts.

Tucker. Tucker. Tucker.

As she slid into his bed next to him, the heat vibrating from his body stunned her. Her core responded instantly, tightening.

He shifted and tucked her up against him, full frontal, allowing her to feel his massive arousal.

She craved to feel him again, buried deep inside her. Where he belonged.

Sliding herself, catlike, up the length of him, she let out a cry of pleasure as he moaned.

Still, he kept himself apart, not impaling her on his hardness, driving her nearly mindless with desire.

"I want you, Tucker," she murmured. "Make love to me."

"Are you sure?" he asked, his voice raw with hunger and need. "You need to be really, really certain. I don't want you to have regrets, especially about—"

She silenced him with a kiss before he could say the

name. For tonight, she wanted nothing to come between them. She'd deal with the other parts of her life and of his, in the morning.

Deepening the kiss, she felt the exact instant when his control snapped. Gasping sharply, he shuddered, pushing helplessly against her. By rolling slightly, she was able to position herself and lift, taking him inside her.

Oh. My. Heaven. Absolute, perfect heaven.

"Don't move," Tucker gritted. "It's been way too long and I don't want—"

Gazing up at him, she let a devilish grin spread over her features before she moved, just the tiniest bit. She felt his body jerk in response.

"Lucy," he warned. "I'm serious."

She didn't care. She needed him now, all of him, one hundred percent.

Starting slowly, she began to move, riding him hard and fast and furious.

He cried out, arching his back, moving with her. She murmured wordless endearments as he became her everything; the center of her existence, life and death and rebirth, exploding simultaneously.

After, they clung to each other, sweaty and sated. She nuzzled his throat, relishing the feel of him, while her heartbeat slowed.

Lucy couldn't think of a time recently, except for Eli's birth, when she'd been happier or more certain. No matter what she gained or lost in this life, this moment proved one absolute truth. Held in this man's arms, she was whole. There could be no other for her, ever.

"I wish you could have been there when Eli was born," she said softly. "His birth was the closest I've ever come to experiencing a miracle."

Shifting his body slightly, Tucker pulled her closer. "Lucy, did Sean help you through Eli's birth or did your mom fly in from New York?"

The edge in his voice told her how difficult this was for him to ask, and also how important.

"Sean helped me. He took the Lamaze classes and was my breathing coach."

Tucker made a sound low in his throat, a sound of pain. They both knew that would have been his place, had he been here.

"I missed you every single second of my pregnancy," she told him.

"And Sean was there to fill in the empty space."

"It wasn't the same," she hastened to say, touched that he seemed to need reassurance. "I promise you, it wasn't."

"I know, I know. Sean was being a good friend."

"That he was," she admitted quietly. "I can't fault him there."

"But still," he persisted. "There's a world of difference from friend to husband. Did you…er, were you and he… intimate?"

"No," she shook her head, honestly glad to be able to tell him the truth about something she'd agonized over for months. "I couldn't. Even kissing him didn't seem right. It felt sort of like kissing my brother, you know?"

"Lucy?" He lifted her chin, making her look at him. His blue eyes were dark with both love and pain. "While Sean might have agreed to wait until you two were married, you wouldn't have been able to postpone it forever. Did you think about that at all?"

"Honestly, I tried not to." She sighed. "In hindsight, I avoided facing the inevitable. Even if you hadn't come back, I don't know if I could have gone through with marrying him. He kept trying to get me to set a date for the wedding and I kept putting it off. I think I was hoping to simply stay engaged until he realized this wasn't how a relationship should be and broke it off."

Turning her face into his neck, she tried to hide, though in reality she knew she couldn't. "I hurt him, Tucker. Sean didn't deserve to be treated this way. I need to apologize to him, if he'll ever speak to me again."

"Shhh," he soothed. "You made a mistake, we all do. He'll be all right."

"I honestly hope so."

He kissed her again and she lost herself in the sensation. When he finally lifted his head, both of their breathing had quickened.

"I've missed you," he rumbled. "More than you can imagine."

"Me, too." Fairly humming with happiness, she let herself drift into a light doze.

They fell asleep like that, wrapped body to body, as though neither ever wanted to let go.

In the morning, Lucy woke pinned under Tucker's arm. She slid out and away from him, and checked on Eli, who lay in his bassinet awake, but silent. His perfect blue eyes gazed up at her, so like his father's that she got a lump in her throat.

Lifting Eli to her, she changed his diaper. Then she nursed him, still humming under her breath from happiness. If she could take away the danger and the rootless feeling, this would be her idea of a perfect morning after a spectacular night.

Once Eli'd been burped, she placed him back in his bed and glanced at Tucker, who still appeared soundly asleep. For a moment, she let her gaze drink him in, reveling in him. The sight of him filled her in a way that she couldn't explain.

Realizing this, she knew she needed to pull herself back a little. Tucker hadn't changed and neither had she. She still wanted more than he'd ever be willing to give. Now that he'd returned to her, she didn't know how she'd bear it if she lost him again. So she needed to begin the process of steeling herself now.

Crossing to the bathroom, she closed the door behind her and turned on the water for a morning shower, loath as she might be to wash Tucker's scent from her body. Oh, she was in deep. This strengthened her resolve. When he woke, she'd tell him she wanted to take things day by day.

The instant the bathroom door closed behind Lucy, Tucker sprang up, grabbing his phone. He waited for the sound of the shower to start before turning it on.

Calling directory assistance, he obtained the number of the Denver branch of the DEA. Once he reached the front desk, he asked to speak to someone who worked with Finn Warshaw.

The woman who answered seemed to be expecting his call. "I'm Agent Burton and I've been assigned most of Finn's case files while he recuperates," she said. "I'm familiar with your name."

"How is Finn doing?"

"He's in a coma. The doctors have given him a fifty percent chance of recovery."

"Meaning…?"

"He could wake or he could not. If he does, he has a long road to travel to regain full health."

She sounded dispassionately professional.

"What do I do now?" he asked, getting back to business.

"Where are you?"

Hesitant to reveal his exact location, he told her simply a motel.

"I see you still have your phone," she said, not pushing for his exact whereabouts, which surprised him. Maybe it was easier on her if she didn't have to worry about where to put him.

"Yes. But the cartel has Finn's. They've called me once."

"Fantastic," she enthused, sounding upbeat for the first time since the conversation had begun. "We'll run a trace on the GPS unit and maybe we can get them that way."

"What about the sting?"

She went silent for a moment. "I'm sorry," she finally said. "That's been canceled. We've lost two agents and nearly lost Finn, the Special Agent in Charge. We're going to make sure you stay safe, but we want you out of the way."

He could hardly believe what he was hearing. "They've attacked my girlfriend and my baby boy. Blown up the safe house where I was staying. And you seriously expect me to shrug and say 'oh, well, no worries?' Come on, lady. Get real."

"Now listen up, Mr. Drover. Either you do as we ask, or we'll have no choice but to take you into custody. I cannot allow you to endanger this investigation."

Taking a deep breath, he willed himself calm. "What about Lucy Knowlton, my girlfriend, and Eli, our son? Finn was going to make sure they were taken to a safe house. Can you arrange that?"

"Mmm." She sounded distracted. "Let me do some

checking on it and I'll see what we can do. I know how to contact you now. We'll be in touch."

And without waiting for a response, she ended the call.

Damn. He resisted the urge to throw the phone against the wall. It sure sounded like the DEA had washed their hands of him, which he found hard to believe.

If he didn't hear from this Agent Burton by this time tomorrow, he'd call again. Next time, he'd demand to speak to her supervisor.

Meanwhile, it appeared they were now on their own.

The shower shut off and he hurried to power down his phone and pocket it. A few minutes later, Lucy emerged, damp-haired and smiling.

"I could eat a horse," she announced. "Hurry up and shower so we can go get breakfast."

Now that was the Lucy he remembered. One of the things he'd admired most about her was her enthusiastic attitude toward life.

Still, he had to make things clear between them before they went any further. "About last night," he began.

He could have sworn a shadow crossed her face. Then, while he was still pondering what that could mean, she nodded.

"I guess you're right. We need to talk about this first thing." Toweling her hair, she moved closer. "Now do you want to go first, or shall I?"

Because he figured she'd simply reiterate her desire for commitment from before his disappearance and he didn't want to hurt her feelings, he elected to start.

"Last night was wonderful," he said. "A dream come true. But I still want you to go to a safe house. And before you say it, no I'm not sending you away from me. I simply want to make sure you and Eli stay safe."

Expression troubled, she bit her lip. "Tucker, before you start in on all that, you need to know that I don't want anything from you. If that's what you're worried about, you can stop. I don't want commitment."

Stunned, at first he couldn't respond. "What do you mean?" he asked carefully. "Are you saying you want to be friends with benefits?"

She frowned. "I wouldn't put it like that." Then she offered him a tentative smile.

"Really?" He was beginning to wonder if he still knew her at all. "How would you put it then?"

Her smile faded as she realized he was not happy with her. "I want to take it one day at a time. We'll see where it goes."

Struggling to take this in, he couldn't help but feel like she was rejecting him. Was this how she'd felt in the past, when he'd brushed off her attempts to solidify their future?

He'd been a fool then. He wanted to rectify that mistake now.

After all, things were completely different. They had a child together. But then she'd said she didn't want to use Eli to tie him to her.

As if she'd need to. They were meant to be, the two of them. It would be up to him to convince her of that.

He glanced at her, with her chin lifted up and defiance sparking her caramel eyes. Maybe subconsciously, she wanted a fight, a way to clear the air and release some tension.

On the other hand, he just wanted to enjoy their remaining time together before the DEA relocated her and Eli to a safe place. After that, he didn't have any idea how long it would be until he saw them again.

Lucy had been surprised at Tucker's reaction to her no-commitment statement. It had taken a lot of courage for her to say it, especially given that it was in direct contradiction to what she'd asked from him before.

Worse, she was still aching from hurting Sean, which she'd never wanted to do. She'd been wrong to accept his marriage proposal in the first place—she saw that now. But he loved her and Eli and she'd crushed his dreams as if he meant nothing to her at all.

Which absolutely wasn't the case.

They'd both have been better off if they'd remained as friends. No expectations, no need to hurt anyone.

And now she'd had to do something similar to Tucker. It couldn't be helped, but still… He'd looked stunned. She'd have thought he'd have been over the moon. After all, she was giving him everything he'd ever wanted, or seemed to want, before he'd gone to Mexico.

Men. She wondered if she'd ever understand them. How could she, when she barely understood her own actions or needs?

Once everything had been completely straightforward. Not so. Ever since Tucker's proverbial return from the dead, life had been a nonstop whirlwind of danger and desire. If she hadn't had a baby to worry about, she might have been able to let herself relax and enjoy the ride.

But she couldn't. She only wanted life to return to normal. Then maybe she could think straight enough to figure out if Tucker could have a place in her life as well as his son's.

* * *

Tucker heard back from Agent Burton more quickly than he'd thought he would. After Lucy's startling announcement, they'd both been uncomfortable, glad to get out of the hotel room and go to breakfast.

While he waited for the waitress to bring his ham and cheese omelet, he sipped a cup of black coffee and turned his phone back on so he wouldn't miss any calls—either from the cartel or the DEA.

Downing a second cup, he started on a third when the waitress brought their food. He'd barely started eating his breakfast when Agent Burton phoned.

"We've arranged a meeting," she said, without preamble. "Our men want those guys badly, so we're going to use you after all. I need you to head into Golden now. There's an Inn near the Coors plant. You're scheduled to meet them there in an hour."

"No," Tucker said simply. "I'm not meeting anyone until you arrange for a safe place for Lucy and Eli."

Silence while she digested this, which was clearly not what she expected. Then, she swore softly.

"Look. You aren't in a position to negotiate." Her clipped tone had turned icy. "I suggest you do as we say."

"Or what? What exactly do you propose to do?"

"For starters, we can arrest you for conspiring to distribute drugs," she threatened. "Obstruction of justice, injury to a federal officer, you name it."

"I had nothing to do with any of that." He had the idea his hot protest fell on deaf ears.

"Maybe not now," she said. "Be at that Inn. Don't let Finn's death count for nothing."

Now she'd shocked him.

"Death?" Stunned, he swallowed hard. "Finn is dead?"

"As of seven forty-three this morning. Someone got past the guards, broke into his hospital room and suffocated him with a pillow."

"I don't understand." Tucker had a hard time accepting the news. "Why would anyone want to do that?"

"We're working on finding that out." Though she sounded assured and competent, something in the way she dismissed his question infuriated him.

"While you are, why don't you work on keeping the body count from rising as well?" He had to throw that out there. "Including me and my family."

"Believe me, Mr. Drover. We are trying."

"Not hard enough. Finn understood that my family's safety is my highest priority and he made it his. You, however, don't seem to give a rat's ass."

She sucked in her breath. "I am doing the best I can. If Finn promised you a safe house for them, he didn't notify us. No provisions were even initiated. I've started the process, but it takes time. First, we have to locate an available place. Next, we have to arrange transport. So believe me, when I say I'm doing all I can, I mean it."

Trying to wrap his mind around Finn's death was hard enough. But hearing from another DEA agent that Finn had lied. Tucker didn't believe her. Plain and simple.

"Now," she continued, apparently taking his silence for contrite embarrassment. "Are you going to be at the Inn or not?"

Stubbornly, he stuck to his guns. "Only if you can protect Lucy and Eli. Until then, no go." Meanwhile, his omelet was getting cold.

She swore. "We don't have time for that. Leave them wherever you're holed up. They'll be safe there."

Right. Finn wasn't safe even in what Tucker assumed had been a heavily guarded hospital room.

"No deal." He hung up on her without waiting for a response.

His phone rang again immediately. Instead of answering, he turned it off without even looking at it. His stomach churned, making him wonder if he'd even be able to eat.

"What happened?" Lucy leaned forward, expression concerned. She put her fork down, her own breakfast only half eaten. "Who died?"

"Finn, the DEA agent I was working with."

"The guy who was attacked outside your safe house?"

"Exactly." He frowned. "The new agent is a woman and she's a regular ballbuster." He relayed what Agent Burton had wanted him to do.

"I'm glad you told her no," Lucy said. "But not because I'm worried about being alone. The more involved I am in this, the more I understand exactly how dangerous these cartel members are. You don't need to go anywhere near them. I don't want anything to happen to you."

Though his omelet had gotten cold, it still tasted great. Scarfing it down without replying, he finished his hash browns and toast. Then, he warmed up his coffee and sat back, checking his phone. "I have one new voice mail. Let's see if she changed her tune."

Replaying his message, he listened with growing shock. When it had finished, he hit the key to make it repeat again.

"Damn."

Lucy eyed him across the table, her caramel gaze concerned. "What's wrong? What'd the DEA do this time?"

"They didn't do anything." Shaken to the core, he gave a heavy sigh. Then, not wanting to worry her, he only told her part of the truth. "The cartel has a hostage." He swallowed hard and met her gaze. "They say they're going to kill him if I don't return the money to them right away."

Chapter 11

Suddenly exhausted, he rubbed his eyes. This was a flipping nightmare.

"What are we going to do?" At least she hadn't asked who.

He looked at her, miserable. "I don't know. Since I don't have the money, there's no way I can do what they ask, even to save him."

"We've got to do something!"

"We will." Pulling his phone back out, he punched in Agent Burton's number. Talk about dealing with the devil. "Maybe the DEA can help. They're our only hope."

But Agent Burton wasn't in a mood to bargain with him.

"You let the entire meeting fall apart," she snarled. "Not only did you endanger my agents' lives by not showing up, but you risked screwing up the credibility of my guy undercover. If you want our assistance, you need to start helping us. You scratch our back and we scratch yours. Get it?"

"Yes." Keeping his tone as level as he could under the circumstances, he took a deep breath. "Though this time, I'm going to agree to a meeting. I have a direct line to the cartel."

"Are you gonna show up this time?" She sounded skeptical.

"Another person's life is on the line, so yes. I'll be there with bells on. Make sure your agents are, too. I'll call you when I know a place and time."

Without waiting for her confirmation, he ended the call. Immediately, he dialed Sean's cell phone, hoping against all hope that the message had been some kind of cosmic mistake and that Sean was safe.

But instead of Sean, an unfamiliar, heavily accented voice answered. *"Bueno."*

"This is Tucker Drover. What have you done with my friend?"

Instead of answering, the other man laughed. "We are done playing your stupid games. You already know we want our money. All of it. Right now. So, you have twenty-four hours to show up with our money. Then, we will trade you. Our money for your friend. A good trade, yes?"

A good trade, his ass. Tucker knew if he were to show up with the cash, both he and Sean were as good as dead. Which would be really difficult to do, considering he didn't have their damn money.

Exasperated, Tucker cursed. "I swear to you, not only do I not have your money, but I have no idea who does or where it is. You've got to let him go."

"We ain't got to do nothing." The other man still

sounded amused. But then, why shouldn't he? At this point, he held all the cards. "It's up to you. You have twenty-four hours. The clock is ticking." And he hung up.

If he'd been alone, Tucker would have been out of luck. Even now, he wasn't sure he could pull this off. The only advantage he had was that he had the DEA to provide backup. Maybe they could supply fake money as well.

Immediately he punched in Agent Burton's number and waited impatiently for her to answer.

Tucker had left, saying only that he was going to meet with the DEA and that she should stay put. He'd reiterated his desire to have her and Eli be taken to a safe house, telling her he could concentrate better if he knew she was safe. Because of that, this time she'd promised to consider it. And she would, because she wanted a future for her baby, herself and Tucker.

She'd even kissed him goodbye, something that in the past when he'd insisted on traveling so much, she'd sworn she'd never do.

Since Eli was asleep and she couldn't exactly leave the room, Lucy had turned on her phone and checked her email. Since she was off work during the summer, she usually didn't have a lot. However, the school district often planned some sort of teachers' educational seminars in the last weeks of the summer and she wanted to check and see if they'd posted the dates yet. They hadn't, but she had a few other emails to read, which she did.

The first call came barely five minutes later, the shrill sound startling her and making her jump.

Sean. Hastily turning the ringer off so it wouldn't

disturb Eli, she ignored the call but left the phone on vibrate, so she'd know in case Tucker tried to reach her.

To her surprise and growing unease, Sean called again in fifteen minutes. Again, she didn't answer.

The time between the next call was only ten minutes. Even after she'd finished checking email and put the phone down, it continued to vibrate. Ten minutes became five. Each time, she had to check the caller ID to make sure it wasn't Tucker.

By the fifth call from Sean, she'd decided this was ridiculous and punched the accept button.

"This better be an emergency," she snapped. "What do you want, Sean?"

"Well, hello to you, too," Sean teased. "Why are you so grouchy? Things not working out with Tucker?"

His lighthearted banter, such a marked difference from the way he'd been last, gave her pause. "Seriously, Sean. You've called five times in the last hour. What's up?"

"Tucker asked me to get you in a safe house," he said, his tone becoming serious. "I made some phone calls per his instructions and it's all set up. The FBI asked me to pick you up for them."

This gave her pause. "The FBI?" she asked slowly. "Don't you mean the DEA?"

"They're working together on this," he replied. "And the danger level has ratcheted up a notch or two. Apparently, things are really heating up. We don't have too much time to get you out of there. Now tell me where you are so I can come and get you."

Something was off, though she wasn't sure what. "Let me call Tucker first," she stalled. "Is he there with you?"

"No. He's not here." Sean sounded surprised that she would even think so. "He was on his way to meet someone. He didn't say whom, just that it was urgent. He just wanted me to pick you up and take you to the FBI offices. One less thing for him to worry about, you know?"

Though Sean had just repeated nearly the exact same phrase that Tucker had used earlier, something still felt off. Why would Tucker involve Sean in this mess? That would be like providing one more person for the cartel to target.

"Let me get back to you," she said, and hung up.

Immediately, she phoned Tucker. The call went right to voice mail, indicating he'd turned off his phone again. Stomach churning, she left a quick message asking him to call her and began to pace, trying to decide what would be the right thing to do.

While she waited for Sean to show up, Lucy hurriedly packed a bag for herself and Eli, making sure to bring a lot of diapers and changes of clothing since she had no idea how long she'd have to stay in the safe house.

Since she still felt uneasy, she also made several attempts to reach Tucker. She got voice mail each time.

By the time Sean knocked, she was a nervous wreck. For the space of a heartbeat, she debated pretending to be gone.

The instant she answered the door and saw Sean standing outside, she had a flash of realization and knew she'd made a mistake. Perhaps it was the way he wouldn't meet her eye or the too-genial way he carried on, but she knew something was majorly off. In a very bad way.

Why? Surely Sean hadn't come on his own, planning to take her back home rather than to a safe house because he wanted to try and get her back.

No, that couldn't be right. Sean clearly understood the danger involved. To all of them.

"Aren't you going to invite me in?" he finally asked, after she stood a moment, studying him in silence.

"Your shirt is buttoned unevenly," she pointed out. "And it's wrinkled."

He glanced down at himself. Then shrugging, he rebuttoned his shirt. "Sorry. I can't do anything about the wrinkles. I left in a big hurry."

While he apparently didn't realize how unusual this was, she did. After all, she'd known him her entire life.

"What have you done?" she whispered.

Cocking his head, he studied her. "I'm only trying to help. Lucy, are you all right?"

"I'm fine. What about you?"

"Better, now that I've found you and Eli. I'm so glad you're all right." He rubbed the back of his neck. "All the tension is really getting to me."

Ah, a semirational explanation. But she still wanted to shut the door in his face and lock it, adding the chain for good measure.

She was being foolish. This was Sean, after all. Chiding herself for being overly dramatic, she summoned up a smile and stepped aside. "Come on in."

Nodding, he stepped inside. He didn't hug her like he normally would have, but she chalked that up to his hurt over her breaking their engagement.

Speaking of… Crossing to her purse, she retrieved the diamond ring he'd given her. "I think you might be wanting this back," she said, handing it to him.

Pain flashed across his face as he accepted it. Pain and something she could have sworn was anger.

For that, she couldn't blame him. She deserved it. "I'm sorry," she said softly. "I never should have accepted your proposal. You deserve better. I promise you, the right one will come along."

He took a step back, almost as if she'd slapped him. "Don't talk down to me. I really don't want to discuss this right now. Just hurry up and get ready."

Still she wavered. "But I hate that I hurt you," she began.

"Obviously not enough not to do it," he shot back, glancing at his watch. "Now, we've got to get out of here. How quickly can you pack?"

"I'll need just a few minutes." She didn't tell him she'd already finished. Alarm bells were going off again. Claiming she had to use the bathroom, she went and checked on Eli, then went inside the restroom and locked the door before trying again to phone Tucker.

Again the call went directly to voice mail. This time she left an urgent message, asking Tucker to call her as soon as he could.

When she emerged, her heart skipped a beat as she saw Sean had taken Eli from his bassinette and held him in his arms.

"He missed me, you know." Smiling at her, Sean raised Eli up onto his shoulder. "He's my little E."

Again, pain stabbed her like a knife to the heart. She really had been an idiot to think Sean would ever hurt them. "You're a good man, Sean Morey. And yes, I believe Eli has missed you. He loves you, you know."

All worries gone, she took Eli from him and strapped the baby into the car seat carrier. While she did this,

Sean grabbed the diaper bag and her own small over-
night case.

"We're ready," she said, swallowing the trepidation
that kept returning. No matter how many times she told
herself that she was being foolish to be afraid, no matter
how often she reminded herself that this was Sean, that
he'd never allow any harm to come to her or to Eli, she
couldn't shake this feeling of unease.

Watching her closely, Sean nodded. Still smiling
that too-wide smile, he opened the door with a flourish.
"After you," he said, his gaze softening as he looked at
Eli.

Outside, the world continued as normal. Cars whizzed
by, birds sang and in the distance she could hear the
sounds of children playing.

"So," Lucy asked casually once she and Sean were
in the parking lot, "are we going to the FBI office in
Denver or are we meeting them somewhere else?"

Once again avoiding her gaze, Sean unlocked the car.
"Neither. We're going directly to the safe house."

Her vague unease returned tenfold. "They told you
where the safe house is?"

"Yep. They're shorthanded after losing all those
agents."

Okay. Hands shaking, Lucy set Eli's carrier on the
ground. She unbuckled Eli and handed Sean the carrier.
"Would you mind setting this up in the back? It doubles
as a car seat."

Waiting while he secured the car seat in the back,
she debated whether to go with him or simply take off
on her own with Eli on foot. But where would she go?
Again, she told herself that this was Sean, after all. One
of her oldest and closest friends. She'd cared enough

about him to agree to marry him once, even though she now knew she'd been misguided.

But her intentions had been good, hadn't they? Plus, Tucker had trusted him enough to tell him where she was. Why shouldn't she?

But still, she couldn't shake the strong feeling of disquiet as she got in his car and buckled herself in. In the relentlessly bright sunlight, Lucy felt foolish to be so worried. Still, she'd never been one to discount her intuition. Since she believed in tackling problems head-on, she'd simply comment.

"Sean, you're acting weird," she said when he'd straightened up after he'd finished getting the car seat securely fastened. Thought she kept a pleasant expression on her face, she held on tight to Eli, not wanting to hand the baby over until she was one hundred percent positive Sean was on the up-and-up.

Meeting her eyes, he gave her a slow smile. "Weird? I'm sorry, but honestly, can you blame me?"

His brown eyes seemed sincere. "What do you mean?"

With a shrug, he dug his car keys from his pocket. "Really, Lucy? You break off our engagement and run off with Tucker and you wonder why I'm acting... weird?"

He had a point. "It's me who should be apologizing to you," she said quietly. "I never wanted to hurt you, but even if Tucker hadn't come back, it wouldn't have worked out between us."

"I disagree. We were happy. We could have made a life together. In time, you would have come to love me more. It would have been enough."

Though she was wary of starting anything, there were things that had to be said. "It shouldn't have been enough, Sean. I love you like a brother, not like a husband. You deserve more than that."

Pain flashed across his patrician features. "Maybe I didn't want more than that." He shrugged, smiling once again. "Don't worry about it. I'll get over this. And as for acting weird, I'm truly sorry if I seem distracted. There's a lot going on," he told her. "I'm worried about Tucker."

While Lucy was, too, she had also known Sean since the third grade. Though they'd all been the closest of friends, she'd seen him angry with Tucker before. He'd never hesitated at venting his frustration and he'd never been the type to keep things inside of him, where they festered away.

Under any other circumstances, he'd have given her an earful on why Tucker didn't deserve her and how she was making the biggest mistake of her life. Even if he didn't believe it one hundred percent, that wouldn't have kept him from saying it.

Ergo, he was keeping something from her. "What is it that you're not telling me?" she asked. "Come on, Sean. Level with me."

"This isn't about us, Lucy. Or even about you and him." Finally meeting her gaze, he gave her a twisted half smile. "Tucker's in danger. Real danger. Though he claimed he doesn't want it, I really think he needs my help. I offered, but he was more concerned about you and E. He said he couldn't concentrate on his own safety until he knew you two were safe."

Hearing Tucker's earlier words spoken now, Lucy finally relaxed. Sean was telling the truth. Tucker had asked him to help out. She was just being foolish, worrying about Sean's intentions. Despite the broken engagement, she knew he cared about her and her son.

He would never let either of them come to harm. If she couldn't trust him, then who could she trust?

Handing over Eli, she watched as he buckled the baby into his car seat. When he'd finished, she got in the car.

A moment later, Sean joined her.

"Can I use your cell phone?" he asked while fitting the keys in the ignition. "I let my battery run down and I need to make a quick call."

"Sure." Pulling it from her purse, she handed it over.

He dialed a number, listened, and then hit the off button. "It's busy. I'll try again in a few minutes," he said, sliding her phone into his pocket instead of returning it.

She had to bite the side of her cheek to keep from requesting it back.

Starting the car, they pulled out. Heading south on Main, to her surprise Sean drove on to the Diagonal Highway. They passed Niwot and the IBM complex, going toward Boulder, which was odd.

"The safe house is in town?" she asked. "Or are we traveling through, taking 36 into Denver?"

"Nope, Boulder it is." Still smiling pleasantly, he shot her a look full of cautious optimism that was so like him she found herself smiling back.

"Where in Boulder?" she asked.

"We're going to my house on Table Mesa. Now, before you say anything, think about it. My house is the last place anyone will think to look for you. Especially since you and I broke up."

Alarm bells going off, she stared at him, not sure if she should pretend to be okay with the idea or argue. Now she knew for certain something was up, because the DEA would never send her there. Which meant Sean was acting alone on his own personal agenda. Whether that included exacting revenge for her jilting him, she wasn't sure. Worse, now she didn't know who to fear more—Sean or the faceless drug cartel.

Or was she being a bit melodramatic? Again, she reminded herself that Tucker had sent him. This was Sean. One of her oldest friends. Even with the broken engagement, she knew he still cared about her and about Eli. Then what the hell?

"Sean?" she matched her carefree tone to his smile. "Does the DEA know about this?"

"Of course," he said. "They couldn't get a safe house ready in time, so they asked me if I'd mind."

Okaaay. Now she knew he was lying. Which meant he was up to no good. Though she had trouble believing Sean would be dangerous in any way, shape or form, she didn't want him to accidentally get Tucker hurt because he insisted on following his own plan.

"Does Tucker know?" she asked casually, trying to figure out how to get her phone back.

"Of course." More lying.

Keeping a pleasant smile, she held out her hand for her cell. "Let me see my phone. Maybe I should call him."

"He's busy right now," Sean said, making no move to hand back the cell. "I don't think you should bother him."

"You're probably right," she agreed. Since he had her phone, she didn't exactly have a choice anyway.

For a minute she stared out the window, watching the familiar scenery flash past and the Flatirons grow closer.

"So what's the plan?" she finally asked, trying to

sound like this was all one fun adventure. Maybe if she could trick him into thinking she was okay with this, she could take him by surprise and figure out a way to make an escape if necessary. Who knew, maybe she was overthinking this. It could be that Sean was taking her to his place simply because he planned to try and talk her into reconsidering breaking off their engagement.

"No plan." His lighthearted reply sounded forced. "Just keeping you and E safe."

There was nothing else she could say to that, so she subsided into silence.

Twenty minutes later they pulled into the driveway of Sean's raised ranch house. Before getting out of the car, she looked around. And ordinary residential street on an ordinary summer day. "Does the DEA have undercover guards watching us? I don't see any. There aren't even any parked cars close to your house."

"Oh, yes," Sean answered, a bit too quickly. "They're all over the place." Then, before she could get there, Sean got out and hurried to the backseat and began unbuckling Eli.

"I can do that," she protested.

"I insist." Smiling at her, he lifted Eli out of the car seat and carried him up the front steps, leaving the car seat in the car. When he turned to see if she was following, she saw a flash of triumph in his eyes and realized that he knew as long as he had Eli, she'd follow him like a sheep.

"Let me get the carrier," she said, more to stall for time than anything else. Hands shaking, she undid the seat buckles and finally lifted the car seat out. Every instinct on high alert, she told herself to calm down.

This was Sean, after all. Just Sean.

First off, she could still be wrong about the entire

situation. Second, even if she wasn't, she didn't think he'd hurt her or the baby. Even if he was furious with her for jilting him, she knew he'd never resort to violence. Sean was about as pacifist as they came.

But still…he'd taken her cell phone and then her son.

Waiting for her just inside, Sean turned as she came up to him, effectively blocking her with his shoulder when she tried to take Eli from him.

"Give me my baby," she said, pleased to hear she sounded firm and unafraid. "Please."

"Not just yet, honey." Still smiling pleasantly, Sean closed and locked the front door. "Come on upstairs. I've fixed up the guest room for you. It's got its own bathroom, so you and E will have all the privacy you need."

When she hesitated, he shook his head. "Fine. Eli and I will go first." He climbed the steps, pausing to smile again at her before turning left to head down the hall.

Heart in her throat, Lucy had no choice but to follow. This was seriously creeping her out.

Though Sean had turned on the overhead light and ceiling fan, the guest bedroom still seemed dark. A moment later, she saw the reason. He had nailed a piece of plywood on the outside of the window, as though the glass had been broken. Clearly it hadn't been, so this was his crude method of ensuring that no one could come in or go out through that window.

Pacifist or no, this wasn't good.

"Sean?" As she turned to face him, he shoved Eli at her, forcing her to drop the infant carrier to keep her son from falling.

"I'll explain later," he said, no longer smiling. He took a quick step back and closed the door. She heard a click as he locked it from the outside, then the sound of his footsteps as he left.

Just in case, she tried the doorknob. Locked. She went back and sat on the bed. Now she understood. Sean had set up this room to be her prison. What she didn't know was how long he would keep her here or why.

Leaning back in her chair, Agent Burton crossed her arms and stared at him. "Is this some kind of a joke? Why didn't you mention the time constraint before? We would have gotten the wheels in motion much faster."

"It never occurred to me. Sorry. I was too worried about my friend, Sean."

"Sean. That's your business partner, right?" she asked.

"Yes," he answered. "The cartel couldn't get to Lucy and Eli, so they grabbed the only other person who means anything to me—Sean."

"What about your parents and siblings?"

"My parents are in Nepal doing missionary work— long story. And I'm an only child."

She nodded. "All right, then. Here's what I want you to do. Call him back and set up a meeting. Tell him you'll bring the money, but only part of it. This will be kind of a good faith thing. In other words, you know if you brought it all, they'd simply kill you and your friend, Sean."

"What about the money? I don't have it."

"There's a bunch of really good counterfeit stuff I have access to. It'll take jumping through too many hoops to get that cleared, so I'm not going to go through proper channels. I'll just use it and worry about the consequences later."

"That'll work. Thanks," he said.

"No thanks are necessary. If things go according to plan, you're going to help me bring down one of the largest and most troublesome drug cartels operating around the Mexican border." She sounded satisfied— and optimistic, which he appreciated.

"Now, we're going to outfit you with a wire," she continued. "You won't be going out there alone by any means, though we're going to make sure they think you are. Meanwhile, you'll be under heavy surveillance."

He thought about it for a moment. "I need to be armed."

Studying him, she narrowed her eyes. "Do you know your way around a firearm? Are you familiar with a pistol?"

"I know how to shoot."

"Then I think in this instance that can be arranged."

That settled, she listened while he made the call to Sean's cell. Again, he spoke to the unnamed Mexican.

When he'd finished, agreeing to meet the representatives from the cartel at an abandoned warehouse in Aurora in two hours, she immediately got on her desk phone, putting together a team.

Then she took him down the hall for her tech people to get him ready.

The DEA people had this type of sting procedure down to a science. Within thirty-five minutes of his arrival in the tech department, they had Tucker outfitted with a wire and commenced giving him instructions on how the operation would proceed.

"We're taking two teams," Agent Burton began. "One to cover the front, the other will go around back. We're going to hit them from both sides and put the squeeze on him."

Tucker nodded, trying to steady his nerves. He couldn't help thinking how reality was different than TV. On television, no one seemed to realize they could get shot and killed.

At least Agent Burton had promised he could have a weapon. This made him feel slightly better about his role in this thing.

"Once we breach, I want you to hit the floor," Agent Burton continued. "No funny business, no heroics, just hit the floor, plain and simple. Can you handle that?"

"Yes, but I want that gun you promised," Tucker responded. "I have to have a way to protect myself."

Giving him a sheepish grin, Agent Burton shook her head. "About that… I've reconsidered. They're going to pat you down for weapons ten seconds after you arrive. There's no way they'll let you keep a pistol, so why waste one?"

About to argue, Tucker realized she was right. "Fine."

Conceding the point, he gestured at his chest, now wrapped tightly in some kind of electrical tape. "Then what about the wire? If they pat me down, won't they find that?"

"That's highly unlikely due to the location." Since the DEA tech guy seemed to know what he was talking about, Tucker left it at that.

Five more minutes and they were ready to hit the road.

"Come on," Agent Burton said. "You're riding with me. You'll let me out five blocks before you reach the warehouse, and I'll ride in with the rest of my team. As a precaution, we're going to circle around and approach from the southeast. We should arrive about ten minutes before the agreed-upon time."

And they were off.

A few short minutes later, Tucker pulled over and let Agent Burton out. Before she left, she studied him, then held out her hand. "My name is Daisy," she said gruffly. "Sorry I was so hard on you earlier."

Surprised, he shook her hand. "No worries, Daisy. Now remember, I'm trusting you to keep me from getting killed or worse, letting them take me captive. I'd rather be shot dead instantly than have to go through that again. Understand?"

She made direct eye contact as she slowly nodded. "Let's hope it won't come to that, all right?" Without waiting for an answer, she got out of the car and shut the door.

He waited until he'd watched her climb into the Tahoe behind him before taking off. He drove around to the back of the warehouse, as he'd been instructed, and parked next to a beat-up, old Chevy van close to the building. The only other vehicles nearby looked as though they'd been parked there permanently and now provided a refuge for wildlife.

Glancing around him for guards and faintly surprised to find none, he went to the metal warehouse door and pulled. Though some of the red paint flaked off in his hand, the door opened with a squeak. Bracing himself, he went inside.

Once the door closed behind him, effectively blocking out the light, he had to stop and let his eyes adjust to the darkness. The briefcase full of counterfeit money felt heavy, though it wasn't. Maybe knowing it contained over a million dollars—even if it was fake—made it feel that way.

A man emerged from the shadows, flicking a switch that turned on several overhead lights. Despite the fact that he wore a ski mask over his face, he looked vaguely familiar. He had a large pistol pointed directly at Tucker.

"Hands in the air," he barked, hand over his mouth to muffle his voice. He spoke completely unaccented English and, despite his obvious attempt to disguise his voice, Tucker recognized it.

"Sean?" he asked, incredulous. "Is that you?"

"Now," the other man ordered, not answering Tucker's question.

His certainty was growing; nevertheless, Tucker did as requested, heart pounding as the man patted him down, praying he wouldn't find the wire.

He didn't.

"You're good," the man said, stepping back. Then, while keeping the gun aimed at Tucker, he pulled off the mask.

Sean, his expression furious, glared at him.

"Damn, Sean. It is you." Suspicions confirmed, Tucker couldn't believe it. "What the hell's going on?"

Staring coldly at him, Sean didn't answer. "This way." He directed with his weapon still pointed at Tucker. "I'll be right behind you."

Walking in the direction he'd been told, Tucker wondered what the listening DEA agents thought of this development. Rather than meeting with the cartel, he was meeting with…Sean?

"I don't get it," he said out loud. Good thing Sean didn't think to check him for a wire. Though Tucker didn't think it would matter either way. Whatever Sean was up to, he was intent and serious.

Tucker tripped on something, stumbling as the empty paint can clattered.

"Keep moving," Sean ordered. "Or I'll put a bullet in your back."

"Come on, man. Get real. Stop this now before someone else gets hurt," Tucker said, pausing and turning to face his friend.

Still holding the gun, Sean glared at him, the hatred burning in his gaze giving Tucker pause. "The cartel will be here shortly," he said. "What the hell do you have in that briefcase?"

"Part of the money," Tucker answered, surprised when Sean's mouth twisted in a bitter smile. "Over a million dollars?"

"Right. Where the hell did you get that? Your accounts are all frozen and I know you don't have the cartel's money."

"You do?" Suspicion dawning, he eyed the man he'd once called his best friend. "And you know this how?"

Returning his look, Sean smirked. "Because I have the money. I've had it all along. Now I don't know where you got that briefcase full of money, but hand it over. Put it on the floor and slide it over to me."

Tucker did as he asked. "Let me get this straight. You stole the money from the drug cartel and you're meeting them here?"

"Correct." Keeping the gun trained on Tucker, Sean knelt and clicked open the briefcase. "Damn." He seemed surprised to find the cash inside. "You were serious."

"Of course I was." Tucker let the bitterness color his voice. "I brought that money because I believed I was rescuing my best friend."

"You're a fool. You always were." Closing the briefcase, Sean stood back up. "The guy you know as

Miguel Gonzalez is on his way here to meet with me. I promised him I'd bring you and the money."

"And what do you get in return?"

Instead of answering, Sean shook his head, his expression once again wild. "Shut up. I refuse to let you screw this up for me. You've taken everything else I had, but you can't have this. This money is mine."

"Sean," Tucker began, trying to sound both reasonable and conciliatory. "Calm down, buddy. I'm not trying to take the money. I just want to know how you stole it and why."

"How is Lucy?" Practically spitting her name, Sean circled around. "And the baby? They were going to be my family, until you showed back up. You couldn't even have the sense to stay dead."

Aware that if he were to respond to this, he'd most likely set Sean off again. Instead, Tucker asked another question. "That money you've brought for Miguel. Is it the entire missing ten million dollars?"

Expression like stone, slowly Sean shook his head no. "But it's enough. He's paying me a finder's fee. Kind of like a bounty." Sean's smile was cold and brilliant. "And don't even think about asking me to cut you in. You've done nothing to deserve it. I've earned it—by bringing you in. The money is all mine. I've got it stashed safely away in an offshore account. It's untouchable now."

Ignoring this, Tucker pressed on. "The drug cartel is foaming at the mouth for that money. DEA agents have been killed because of it."

"Not my problem."

Suddenly, Tucker couldn't stand pretending anymore. This man, rage darkening his eyes and twisting his features, bore no resemblance to his childhood best friend. "What the hell is wrong with you? You've changed. What happened to you, Sean?"

Sean froze. Then he laughed, a mirthless sound full of bitterness. "What happened? Funny that you should have to ask. You're what happened." Venom dripped from every word. "All our lives, you've been the first, the best and the brightest. I only got in on starting up BBB because you let me. Everything I've ever done, every accomplishment, has been because of you. You've always dropped me your leavings."

"That's not true," Tucker interjected.

Ignoring him, Sean continued. "You even took Lucy from me. I've loved her since third grade, but she only had eyes for you."

Touchy subject. "The money, Sean." Steering the conversation back on track, Tucker kept his voice calm and level. Though he had a feeling he wasn't going to like Sean's answer. "I refuse to believe you originally stole it. You didn't even go to Mexico with me, so you couldn't have been initially involved in this. How did you happen to get hold of the drug cartel's mission money?"

Sean's laugh sent chills up Tucker's spine. "Not involved? Dude, I'm the one who orchestrated the entire thing. Bruno came to me with a business proposition. We could steal the money, as long as we could make it appear someone else did. You happened to be going to look at coffee beans at the right time to make it appear you were the thief. So that's what we did. As far as the cartel is concerned, you and Carlos stole their money."

Stunned, for a moment Tucker couldn't speak. When he did, all he could do was tell Sean something he most likely already knew. "Carlos is dead."

"Yep." Sean's expression remained unchanged. "And they were supposed to kill you, too. I'm guessing they figured if they tortured you long enough, you could tell them where you'd hidden their money."

Tucker's blood ran cold. His childhood best friend, the man he'd thought of as a brother, had just admitted arranging Tucker's death. "Only I couldn't tell them where the money was, since I didn't know," he said slowly.

"Correct," Sean said, his broad smile contrasting with his dark gaze. "It should have only been a matter of time before they broke you or accidentally killed you. I was surprised you lasted so long. I figured you'd die in captivity."

The horror of having a man he'd grown up with and once considered his best friend say such a thing had Tucker wincing with pain. But then, he realized with a growing sense of shock, that meant Sean had known all along that he wasn't dead. In fact, had he wanted to, Sean could have rescued him and shortened his stay in hell.

Sean could have saved his life, but he'd chosen not to.

Not only that, but he'd let Lucy mourn for nothing, aware all along that Tucker was very much alive and being held captive in Mexico.

And that wasn't even the worst of it.

The fact that he had *caused* all of Tucker's suffering, relished it and planned to celebrate by cashing in on the very money the cartel still believed Tucker had stolen was damn near unbelievable.

Sean meant to serve him up to the cartel on a silver platter.

Tucker remembered Agent Burton's instructions to

stall. That didn't seem to be a problem as Sean appeared to be enjoying gloating. Still, he figured the other man could use a little prodding.

"Then why this?" Tucker spread his arms. "Pretending you'd been captured and that the drug cartel was going to kill you? What's the point?"

"The point?" Sean smirked. "Is that this time, when you die, I can make sure you stay dead."

"You're not acting alone. I remember you had another man, the one that talked to me on the phone and pretended to be from the drug cartel."

"Bruno." Sean shook his head. "Too bad about him. He's dead."

"You killed him?"

"No, though I might have if he'd gotten greedy. But the cartel got a hold of him. They thought he was your accomplice."

"You won't get away with this," Tucker warned. "The cartel got Bruno and once they figure out you stole their money, they'll be coming after you."

"Ah, but you're wrong." Sean smiled, full of malice. "That's where you come in. They want retribution so badly that they're offering a reward. Like I told you, it's sort of a bounty, and I'm the bounty hunter. I'm going to offer you up—dead—and they're going to pay me three million in cash. I'm told they consider it a small price to pay to get back their seven million and the one who stole it."

"They won't pay you. You forget who you're dealing with. They'll want to keep all of their money."

"Yeah?" Appearing unconcerned, Sean studied his fingernails. "I'm not surprised that you think that. But they've been very adamant about paying the bounty. There are probably six or seven professional bounty hunters looking for you, because the cartel will pay the agreed amount."

"That doesn't make sense."

"Yes, it does. Apparently, they want their revenge almost as much as they want their money. Bad for you, good for me. In fact," he said, looking up and grinning. "It's a win-win. I get it all and lose nothing."

Nothing. His former best friend and business partner had just relegated him to nothing. Obviously, since he'd been willing to let Tucker languish away in a Mexican prison for a year without even attempting to rescue him. That hurt more than he would have believed possible.

"Was it worth it, Sean? Selling out your best friend and the woman you professed to love?"

"Was it worth it, Tucker?" Sean mimicked. "Screwing over your best friend for a piece of tail? You never wanted me to have anything. You always wanted first grab, first choice. In high school, you were the quarterback, and I was the kicker. In college, you made the Dean's list and I didn't."

Tucker had worked hard to earn those accomplishments. But he held his tongue as Sean continued.

"Then, when we started BBB, naturally you were CEO while I was second. Around you, I could never measure up. How do you think that made me feel?" He shook his head, staring at Tucker with narrowed eyes. "Not good, I can assure you. I nearly won once, when the cartel believed they'd captured their thief and Lucy was convinced you were dead. I had it all then."

"Then I escaped and came home."

"Exactly. Once again, you managed to claw your way out and back to the top. Well, now the tables are turned. I'll come out ahead and you'll be the loser for once. Even better, you won't be able to rectify the situation this time. You'll be dead. And I'll get Lucy back. She and Eli will be my family, not yours."

Tucker tried another tact. "What about her, Sean? Do you really want her to learn the truth about you? Once she does, I can promise you she won't want anything to do with you."

Sean smirked. "She won't have a choice in the matter, because she's coming with me, willing or not."

Frowning, Tucker studied his opponent. He didn't like the way Sean sounded so confident. "First you'll have to find her."

"Shows how much you know." Positively gleeful, Sean strolled around the room, chest puffed up like a king surveying his serf. "I've already located Lucy. I picked her up an hour ago, while you were cooling your heels waiting for my supposed captors to show. She and Eli are with me. And, if she wants the baby to live, she'll do exactly as I ask."

Chapter 12

Horrified, Tucker tried to determine if Sean was serious or just…plain crazy.

Sean appeared to sense his skepticism because his self-satisfied grin widened. "You don't believe me?"

"No," Tucker answered carefully. "Not exactly."

"Want proof? Fine. You left her at that motel in Longmont. Room 226."

Tucker's heart dropped. "How?"

"Very simple, my friend. I called her and arranged to pick her up. She came with me very willingly, once I explained to her that you'd asked me to take her to a safe house."

Tucker nearly groaned out loud. If only he hadn't worked so hard to convince Lucy that doing exactly that would be in her best interest. Sean knew him too well and apparently had been able to anticipate his every move.

Still, he wasn't entirely sure that she would have gone with Sean so willingly. "If you really have her, call her. Let me talk to her. That's the only proof I'll accept."

Silence while Sean pondered his request. Then, "Right. Like you let me talk to her when I wanted to. No go, my friend."

"I'm not your friend."

Sean ignored the interruption. "Besides, not only does she not have a phone, but even if I were foolish enough to leave her a method to communicate with the outside world, I wouldn't want to alert her that anything was wrong. No sense in getting her all worked up. She probably isn't even aware she's in danger."

"Is she?" Latching on to Sean's last word, Tucker clenched his jaw. "In danger, that is?"

Smiling broadly, Sean shook his head. "No. Not yet."

Not yet. Which could mean a thousand things. Or nothing. He hated that he couldn't tell if Sean was bluffing. Once, he would have known instantly. But Sean had changed and so had he. "Where is she now?" he gritted out.

"Try again. You know I'm not going to answer that."

"Is she okay? At least tell me she's all right."

Sean snickered. "Ah, you don't like it too well when the shoe's on the other foot, now do you? How's it feel, buddy? How's it feel to be the loser this time?"

Ignoring the rhetorical question, Tucker asked his again. "Answer me, damn you. Where are Lucy and Eli? Are they okay?"

Chuckling, clearly enjoying himself, Sean made him wait. When he finally spoke, he drew the answer out. "Yes, of course they're fine. I wouldn't hurt them and you know it. While Lucy has no doubt noticed that the room I've put her in is locked and she can't leave, she probably thinks it's for her own protection."

"Are you sure about that? Lucy is an intelligent woman."

"True." Sean sighed, then continued. "But she knows how I feel about her, so I'm sure she believes I'm only trying to keep her safe."

"How do you feel about her?" Tucker watched him closely. "If you really love her, you'd give her the chance to make her own choice."

"Are you serious? Like that pithy bumper sticker about if you love something, you set it free? You're crazy. Lucy is mine and I'm not letting her go. She's probably quite happily watching TV. Or taking a nap. You know how she is. Always looking for the positive side of things."

"Is there, Sean?" Tucker asked tiredly. "A positive side to all this?"

"Of course." Sean appeared surprised that he'd asked. "It's actually amusing to me that Lucy honestly believes that I'll bring you to her when this is all over. I don't really get how she can think I wouldn't mind her jilting me so that the two of you can get back together."

"You can't change that."

"Uh, yes I can. Once you're dead again, she'll come back to me. Oh, how we'll mourn your passing. She'll think I miss you as much as she does. After all, you and I are best friends."

"No. We're not."

Sean continued as though Tucker hadn't even spoken. "Once you're dead, it'll be entertaining to see how long I can get her to continue to believe that delusion."

"You're a pretty good actor, aren't you?"

"Oh, yeah." Clearly pleased with himself, Sean's expression radiated glee. "And neither you or she is. She'll believe just about anything I tell her."

Clenching his fists, Tucker had to struggle to keep his voice level. "Like when you convinced her to believe I was dead for an entire year when you knew damn well I wasn't?"

Sean raised one brow. "Such bitterness. I'd hate for you to have to live with that festering inside you. It's a good thing you're going to die soon. I'm actually doing you a favor, you know? Guess I'd better get those events in motion."

Sauntering over to the table, he picked up a cell phone and dialed a number. "I have him," he said into the receiver. "And even better, he has your money with him. It's all good, no problems. Exactly as I promised. When do you want to meet?"

Since Sean hadn't checked him for wires, Tucker knew the DEA was getting every word. He also knew they wanted the cartel as well or more than they wanted Sean, so they wouldn't make a move until acutely necessary.

He hoped that would be before Sean killed him. Since Sean apparently planned to bring his dead body to the meeting with the cartel, he'd have to convince him otherwise.

Swallowing, he eyed the other man, his patrician features and buttoned-up look exactly the same as they'd been when they were kids. He couldn't help wondering when Sean had gone off the deep end and how he had missed this. A change of this magnitude took years to develop.

"Where do you want to meet? Here?" Sean checked his watch, appearing a bit uncertain. "That will be fine.

The sooner the better. I'm looking forward to doing business with you. *Ciao*."

Looking smug, he finally ended his call. "All set," he said cheerfully. "It looks like my ship is about to finally come in. And even though I hate to admit it, it's all thanks to you."

What the hell? This was the man he'd thought of as his right arm, his best friend. He'd have thrown himself in front of a bullet if it'd meant saving his life and he'd have sworn Sean would have done the same. Once. Apparently, not now.

Staring at the man who'd become his worst enemy, he tried to reconcile the two. He couldn't reconcile the memories of their childhood, the high school and college years after, during which they'd remained close friends, and starting BBB together. They'd been as close as brothers.

Now this? Sean actually despised him and the hate had festered inside, making him deadly and insane. How had he missed the signs? Maybe he simply hadn't wanted to see them.

"Are you ready?" Sean grinned at him. "This is going to be fun."

"So you're going to do what?" Tucker asked. "Turn me over to Miguel so they can torture me as retribution before they kill me?"

Sean cocked his head, the question appearing to amuse him. "Nope. I'm going to kill you myself, like I should have done the first time. That way I can make sure you're really dead."

The first time? Ignoring this, Tucker prayed his plan would work. "Thank you, buddy. I can't tell you how much I appreciate that." Tucker managed to sound grateful. "Despite how you pretend to despise me, I know you still care. I'd a thousand times rather die quickly than go through what they did to me last time. Thank you so much."

While Sean stared at him he gave an exaggerated shudder, and then added for good measure. "And I know whatever they did to me would be a thousand times worse now, especially since they really think I actually stole their money. They'd want to draw out their revenge slowly. They'd want to make me suffer for retribution."

He could see the wheels turning as Sean mulled this over. If he was as crazy and hated Tucker as much as he appeared to, then he'd relish the idea of Tucker suffering at the cartel's hands.

"You know what," Sean finally said, eyeing him coldly. "Now that you've pointed that out to me, I think I've changed my mind. I'm going to keep you alive. I think I'll let the cartel have the pleasure of killing you. I'd enjoy knowing you'd be suffering. Plus, you'd probably be much more valuable to them alive rather than dead."

Tucker struggled to look dismayed and terrified. He couldn't believe Sean had been so easy to sway. Crisis averted, at least for now.

Until the cartel members arrived. Then they'd be playing with an entirely new ball of wax.

When the exterior door to the warehouse clanged open, Sean jumped and then shrugged, grinning broadly. "Ah, that must be your pal, Miguel," he said, sounding satisfied. If he hadn't been holding a gun on him, Tucker thought Sean would have rubbed his hands together with glee. As it was, he could barely contain himself.

"Miguel, over here," Sean called. He took a step

forward, looking toward the door, the gun wavering slightly from Tucker's chest.

With Sean distracted, Tucker saw his chance. He charged the smaller man, slamming into him full in the chest and taking him down. Sean managed to squeeze off a shot, but it went wild, ricocheting off a concrete pillar.

"You son of a—"

Tucker knocked the gun out of his grasp before he could squeeze off a second shot, sending it skittering across the cement floor. Sean cursed again, swinging wildly at him as they both dove for it. His fist only glanced off Tucker's shoulder. Defending himself, Tucker landed a solid punch, connecting with Sean's jaw, sending him reeling back into the wall.

Unfortunately, during the scuffle his foot hit the gun and knocked it away, out of reach.

"Hold it right there," a heavily accented voice demanded. Tucker looked up to find the man he'd seen in Boulder—the man he knew as Miguel Gonzalez—holding a gun aimed at his head.

Damn. Glancing at Sean's weapon, still only a good three feet away, Tucker tried to decide whether or not to go for it.

"Don't even think about it," Miguel said. "Unless you want to die instantly."

Tucker froze, holding up his hands.

"That's what I thought." Miguel gestured at Sean, who'd started to get up. "That goes for you, too."

As Sean froze, sputtering a protest, Miguel spoke in Spanish to one of the heavyset men accompanying him, who nodded and turned his weapon, a dangerous looking AK47, on Sean.

"Both of you, hands where I can see them, up against the wall," Miguel directed.

"Come on, Miguel. It's me," Sean protested. "There's no need to—"

"Shut up."

Immediately, Sean did as he'd been directed. For someone who'd plainly been well aware of the ruthless unpredictability of the drug cartel, he seemed surprised by his sudden treatment as an enemy.

Once they both stood up against the concrete wall, facing them, Miguel's goons lined up, weapons trained on Tucker and Sean as though they were a firing squad.

"Now. Where is our money?" Miguel asked. Tucker couldn't help but notice that he frequently glanced at another, silver-haired man, one of the five or six who made up the group accompanying him and the only one who wasn't holding a semi-automatic, machine-gun-type weapon. The look was one of deference, as if Miguel looked to him for direction.

A second later, Tucker realized why. Miguel was only posing as the leader. The older man to whom he deferred was clearly the one giving orders, albeit silently.

"The money," Miguel repeated. "Where is it?"

"I have it," Sean answered, licking his lips nervously. He pointed at Tucker. "And I brought you this man as you wanted. He's the one who robbed you in the first place."

"That's a lie," Tucker declared, seeing his chance to invalidate Sean. "Don't believe a word he says. He stole your money and set it up to make it look like I did. Like I've been telling you all along, I'm innocent."

Miguel, posing as the drug kingpin, barely spared him a glance. The older man, the true boss, said something in Spanish again to Miguel, who glanced from Sean to Tucker and then back again.

"I should shoot you both, just to be done with it," he said, frowning. "You were very stupid to meet us here. You should know we don't normally pay ransom money to regain what is already ours. We simply kill and take what we want."

From the shocked look on Sean's face, this possibility had never occurred to him. "But you put out the word on the street that you were paying a bounty," he protested. "I did as you wanted, brought the thief and the missing money. I deserve to be rewarded."

"Perhaps. But we've yet to see our money. Produce it."

Sean pointed at Tucker's briefcase. "I have over one million dollars in cash there, in that case."

Miguel made no move to inspect it. "And the rest?"

Lifting his chin, Sean pretended bravado. "Some of it's here. The rest is hidden. As you mentioned, I had to have some kind of insurance to prevent you from simply killing me and taking the money."

Clearly not pleased, Miguel cocked his head. "So you think to double-cross us? I will have you shot. Where is the rest of our money?"

Before Sean could reply, the warehouse door clanged open.

"DEA," a voice shouted. "Drop your weapons and put your hands in the air."

Instead, Miguel's group formed a protective circle around the older man, their guns at the ready. This action served to confirm Tucker's suspicions as to who was the real leader.

Moving as one, the group turned to face the threat. Sean saw his opportunity and grabbed the briefcase with the counterfeit in it. He darted away, into the unlit bowels of the warehouse. Several of the Mexicans shot at him, but apparently they all missed.

Not good. Hearing the shots, the DEA agents returned fire. One man went down. Another, clearly wounded, continued to shoot.

Damn it. Now or never. Muttering a quick prayer, Tucker dove for Sean's gun. Once he had it, he rolled and leapt behind a stack of huge metal containers, using this for cover. Hoping the wire would catch him, he spoke quietly, informing the DEA of Sean's escape toward the back. The gun battle raging around him drowned out some of his words.

Advancing, the DEA continued to shoot. The cartel members continued to return fire, still focusing on protecting their true leader with their bodies. They had to know they weren't going to make it out of this alive. Still, they fought with the cold, ruthless efficiency of trained snipers, with no thought for personal safety, intent on saving their leader.

They were remarkably effective, keeping the DEA from getting too close.

Maybe he could help. Peering around the metal container, Tucker aimed and shot. He scored a direct hit, taking out one man. One of the fallen man's companions returned fire, but Tucker ducked back behind his shield and wasn't hurt.

As the DEA advanced in bits and pieces, step by step they forced the cartel back. Another man was hit in the belly. He cried out in Spanish and fell to his knees, but continued to return fire up until the moment he died.

Damn. Dedicated bunch, these cartel guys. He wondered if the DEA had sustained any casualties.

Ducking out to take another shot, Tucker wondered

where the hell the other DEA team was, the ones that were supposed to come in from the back and squeeze the cartel in a vise.

A moment later he heard gunfire from the direction Sean had run and he knew. Any moment now, they should enter the gun battle and help turn the tide in their direction.

"DEA. Drop your weapons now! Hands up. Now!" As the second group of DEA agents rushed from the back of the warehouse, it was over. Guns clattered on concrete as the remaining Mexicans surrendered. Tucker dropped his pistol, too, and raised his hands, not wanting to be shot by mistake.

Stepping out from behind his metal container, he kept his hands in the air. Spying Agent Burton shepherding a handcuffed Sean before her, he ran over. Sean shot him a rage-filled look, which he ignored.

"We got them." Agent Burton flashed him a satisfied smile. "One of these guys is really high up in the cartel hierarchy. You can relax now, Drover. It's finally over and you're safe."

"It's not over yet." Grabbing Sean by the front of his shirt, Tucker yanked him up until they were nose to nose. "Where are Lucy and Eli?" he demanded.

Despite the nervous perspiration running down his face, Sean merely laughed. "You'll never find them now."

"What's this?" Agent Burton asked, making no move to force him to release Sean.

Tucker filled her in, finally pushing Sean away. The other man, still handcuffed, stumbled. Agent Burton motioned to someone and two men with the letters DEA emblazoned in white on the back of their vests, came and led Sean away.

"You have no idea where your girlfriend and baby are?"

"No." Tucker swallowed. "As you heard, Sean claims to have them stashed somewhere. They're locked in a room. He wouldn't say where."

Barking orders into a walkie-talkie, she had her men search the warehouse. "If they're here, we'll find them."

But a complete search turned up no sign of Lucy or little Eli. Sean still refused to cooperate. The DEA dispatched an agent to check the hotel in Longmont. He'd reported back that while the rented room was empty, there'd been no signs of a struggle.

No surprise there, since Lucy had gone with someone she considered a friend.

Praying she'd kept her cell phone with her, Tucker dialed Lucy's number, hoping against hope that she'd answer.

Chapter 13

Even in custody, Sean refused to speak, beyond requesting an attorney. Watching from behind the two-way mirror as he was questioned, Tucker tried not to get too frustrated by his lack of response. The blank look in his eyes made Tucker think he'd checked out mentally. Sean had adopted a sullen, vacant silence that even the tough Agent Burton couldn't crack. And not from lack of trying.

Finally, she left him in the interrogation room alone.

"As you can tell, he's not talking," she said, entering the viewing room and looking disgusted. "Not about the money or about your girlfriend and baby. We've sent a team to search his home and where he works. Those are both good starting places."

"The Boulder's Best Brew offices? You're wasting

your time. He said he'd convinced Lucy he was taking her to a safe house. He wouldn't have gone there."

She shrugged. "We'll check there, anyway. And I've got people checking to see if he owns any other properties or has rented or leased a house or an apartment anywhere in the Denver metro area or the foothills."

"Thank you," he said.

Winking at him, she smiled. "No base left uncovered and all that."

Staring at her, he shook his head. "You sound so blasé."

"Sorry. I mean no harm. But they'll turn up eventually, completely unharmed. I doubt he put them anywhere they won't be found."

"How do you know this?" He wasn't sure he bought the cop intuition thing.

Agent Butler eyed him, as though she knew what he was thinking. "Because he doesn't fit the profile. We aren't dealing with some sociopathic serial killer here. He didn't want to hurt her or the baby. He just wanted to keep them away from you."

"I don't know," he argued. "He not only arranged the theft of ten million dollars but set me up to look like the guy who stole it. He knew the cartel was torturing me, but made no move to stop it. Instead, he let everyone— including Lucy—believe that I was dead. That sounds pretty psychopathic to me."

"Hey, I didn't say he was a good person." Cuffing him on the arm, she grimaced. "No doubt about that. But believe me, he's not the type to have buried her in a shallow grave or anything. She'll turn up soon. It's just a matter of us finding her."

He got up, heading toward the door.

"Where are you going?"

Surprised, he stopped and turned. "To look for her."

"In a minute, hotshot. We've got to ask you a couple of questions first. For the record."

"Can't that wait until later?"

"Not unless you want to blow the entire case." She sounded grim. "I promise you, my people are working with local law enforcement. We are doing everything we can to find Lucy and Eli. I just need ten minutes of your time."

"Fine." For now, he conceded the point. "What about the cartel guys? Do you extradite them to Mexico?"

"Nope. For this kind of situation, the U.S. has an agreement with the Mexican government. They'll face charges here." She gave him a long look. "You know you'll have to testify."

"I will." Dragging his hand through his hair, Tucker fought back exhaustion. "Send your men in to question me. The sooner we're done, the sooner I can go find Lucy and Eli."

"Take it easy." She crossed to a wall phone, picked it up and spoke into it. "They're on the way. Remember, we've got people searching."

Both of them knew that was not enough.

Two men entered the room. They nodded at Agent Burton, who took a seat against the wall, away from the table. One man placed a notebook on the table in front of him. "Take a seat," he told Tucker.

True to what Agent Burton had told him, the deposition took nine minutes. Less than ten, as she'd promised. When they'd finished, the two men left and Agent Burton stood.

"You're free to go now," she said.

"Thank you." He pushed back his chair. "I'll find her," he swore. As he began to walk away, Agent Burton's cell phone rang. Tucker turned and waited, hoping against hope that Lucy had been found.

Agent Burton answered and listened, motioning to Tucker to wait. Heartbeat kicking into overdrive, he did. Impatiently.

When she finally closed the phone, and gave him a broad smile, he knew. "Lucy and Eli?"

"Yes. They've been found," she said. "My agents were able to locate them both at Sean's house. He had them locked in an upstairs bedroom."

Dizzy with relief, he closed his eyes for a millisecond. "Thank God. Are they all right?"

"Yes. The paramedics checked them out and both are okay. Lucy has requested to be taken home." Her smile widened and she winked. "So if you want to see her, that's where she'll be. We took the liberty of having your car brought around. It's waiting outside. One of my agents will meet you with the keys."

Tucker already had his hand on the doorknob before she'd even finished speaking. He took the stairs to the parking garage two at a time.

The beat-up, old, red Honda parked at the curb looked out of place in this upscale area of Denver. Still, just seeing the car made him smile, because it reminded him of how he and Lucy had taken refuge in it. Another DEA agent got out of the car and handed him the keys. To his relief, the engine started right up, with a hacking growl rather than a purr.

Pulling from the parking spot, he merged with traffic and soon he was on the freeway, heading northwest.

Traffic on I25 going out of Denver at rush hour moved at a crawl. Lost in his own thoughts, he missed the exit for the toll road and got stuck in the middle lane. It took over fifteen minutes to travel one mile.

By the time he exited on 36, he seethed with frustration and a kind of cautious impatience. Until he saw Lucy and Eli, touched them, he couldn't entirely believe they were all right.

Picturing their reunion, he couldn't help but wonder. Now what? Since learning Sean had grabbed her, he hadn't thought much beyond rescue, and before that he hadn't allowed himself to make much in the way of plans.

Though he knew Lucy would welcome him, how would she define their relationship now? Suspecting he knew, he couldn't help but think how odd it was that their roles were now reversed.

He'd been a fool. No two ways around it. Although he'd always loved her, he'd taken her love for granted. Not wanting to be tied to anything or anyone, he'd brushed off her desire for commitment with vague promises and assurances that they'd talk later. Even as he purchased her an engagement ring in Mexico, he'd never once thought about the possibility that there might not always *be* a later.

Now he knew better and could see clearly what he wanted. Unfortunately, he'd hurt her badly. Though neither could imagine a future without the other in it, he knew she was afraid to risk her heart again.

With the wisdom he'd gained in his trials by fire, he knew there was no such thing as love without risk. She'd have to accept that, if she wanted to try for a future as a family.

He could clearly see what he wanted from her. Knew it without a shadow of a doubt. He wanted…everything. He could only hope he hadn't realized this truth too late.

The FBI agents who'd broken down the door had told her Sean was in custody. Though she'd asked repeatedly about Tucker, no one had been able to tell her anything. Over her objections, they'd had paramedics examine both Eli and her. Once they'd been checked out and pronounced fine, she'd insisted that they take her home.

Though the agent who drove her tried to make small talk and seemed very nice, she had no interest in chatting. Since the ride from Sean's place to hers only took a few minutes, she didn't have to.

When they'd pulled up in her driveway and she'd climbed out of the car, she'd brushed aside his attempt to help her remove the car seat, doing it herself. She didn't want to tell him she had to keep busy to keep from weeping.

The agent insisted on coming inside with her and performed a cursory inspection of her home. Once he'd pronounced it clear, he took his leave, pressing his business card into her hand and telling her to call if she needed anything. She'd smiled and nodded and lied, promising she would.

After he'd left, she'd carefully locked her front door. Then, still wanting to keep busy, she'd walked her entire house, feeling an irrational need to check every nook and cranny herself. Once she'd determined her home was safe—though from what, she didn't know exactly—she put Eli in his playpen in the middle of the living room floor and sat down on the couch.

She didn't understand why she felt like the slightest thing would cause her to break, shattering into a thousand pieces. She didn't get why she wanted to cry when she should be rejoicing.

According to the DEA, everything could return to normal. Members of the Mexican drug cartel had been arrested, as had Sean. Whether or not the money had been recovered, she didn't know or really care. As long as Tucker was safe. That was all that mattered.

And normal. What, exactly, was normal? She didn't much know anymore.

Unable to sit still for long, she got up and began to pace. Where was he? She longed to call him, just so she could hear his voice, but she still didn't have her cell phone and she didn't have his cell number memorized.

Pacing, she was so lost in her thoughts that she nearly missed the familiar, battered, red car pulling up in the driveway. Her heartbeat went into overdrive and she tried not to hyperventilate.

But every pore, every cell screamed his name.

Tucker.

Tucker.

Willing herself to calm—and failing miserably—she watched from her front window as he got out of the car and headed up the sidewalk.

She debated letting him ring the doorbell, trying to picture herself calmly walking to the front door and slowly opening it. As if.

Unable to stand still another moment, she said the hell with it and raced to get there before he pressed the bell.

"Hey," she said, yanking the door open. Her voice only trembled a little.

"Hey." He froze, staring at her with a potent mixture of longing and wariness in his blue gaze.

She didn't hesitate—she held out her arms. "Welcome home," she said. And then she kissed him, letting him know that at long last, he had come back where he belonged.

When he finally lifted his head and looked at her,

her heart turned over at the tenderness in his eyes. She flushed as she realized they'd been locked in a passionate embrace practically on her front doorstep.

Her blush deepening, she led him by the hand into the house, closing and locking the door behind them.

"Not taking any chances," she said at his questioning look. "Sorry."

"Ah, Lucy, don't be." He smoothed back the hair from her face. "I'm so glad you're all right."

"Why wouldn't I be?" she asked, reaching up and tracing the worry lines, wanting to erase them from his face. "Sean might have been a bit misguided in his intentions, but you know he would never have hurt me or Eli."

Instead of answering right away, he leaned over the playpen and kissed the downy fluff on Eli's head. Her heart turned over in her chest. Would she ever get used to this sight? The other half of her soul and their son, the two males she loved most in this world?

"There's something I have to tell you," they both began at the same time.

"You first." One corner of his mouth kicking up in the beginning of a smile, he gestured for her to precede him.

Leading him to the couch, she sat, pulling him down next to her. "After you came back from the dead, I thought I'd need time alone, both to sort out things in my head and to prove to myself that I could make it on my own." Her voice broke as her throat clogged and tears prickled at the back of her eyes.

"And now," he prodded gently, when she didn't continue.

She took a deep breath, struggling to keep her composure. "Now, having lost you once and then, after you miraculously returned, damn near losing you a second time, I don't want to waste another moment denying what my heart knows is an absolute truth. I love you and want to be with you. Every single moment we can."

"And if I want more?"

Though she'd told herself it didn't matter, still his question had the power to hurt. "You've never lied to me, Tucker. I'm grateful for that." Searching his face, she couldn't read his eyes. "Whether you want more or not is no longer the issue. I just want you."

"You misunderstand." He caressed her hand with his thumb. "I meant if I want more, are you going to run away as fast as you can?"

"I…" she began, slightly confused and a lot overwhelmed. She caught her breath and her heart skipped a beat as his incredibly blue gaze captured hers. His eyes were full of love.

The question she saw in them made her chest hurt.

When he dropped to one knee in front of her, still holding her hand, at first she was afraid to let herself understand. Then, when he pulled his old class ring from his pocket, the very same ring she'd worn on a chain around her neck for so long, she thought her chest would burst from joy.

"Will you marry me, Lucy Knowlton? I'd love for you to be my wife." He kissed her hand, a lingering tender kiss. "Not only can I not live without you, but you're already the mother of our son." His expression turned mischievous. "Though we're already the perfect family, I'd love to have a couple more children with you someday, if you want."

Staring at him, she couldn't find her voice. Amazing how the world could change in an instant. She remembered with stark clarity, the day she'd learned of his supposed death. She'd fallen to the ground, feeling as though the words had somehow reached inside her, to her core, and ripped out her gut.

Then, to have a second chance. She'd never doubted his love for her, just whether that love would be enough if he didn't want the same kind of life as she did.

And now, for him to offer this, everything she'd ever wanted…

She couldn't help it. Though she tried to hold back her tears, she began to cry.

Expression agonized, he pulled her to him. "Ah, sweetheart, don't cry. I know you didn't like me gallivanting to the four corners of the earth whenever I had the whim."

Wiping at her eyes, she shook her head. "I don't want you to have to give that up for me."

"Give it up?" Hand under her chin, he raised her head and made her look at him. "Who said anything about giving it up? I still want to travel, but I want you and Eli to go with me. Though I think we'll stay out of Mexico for a while."

And just like that, he turned her tears to laughter.

* * * * *

Harlequin

ROMANTIC
SUSPENSE

COMING NEXT MONTH

Available June 28, 2011

#1663 JUST A COWBOY
Conard County: The Next Generation
Rachel Lee

#1664 PRIVATE JUSTICE
The Kelley Legacy
Marie Ferrarella

#1665 SOLDIER'S LAST STAND
H.O.T. Watch
Cindy Dees

#1666 SWORN TO PROTECT
Native Country
Kimberly Van Meter

You can find more information on upcoming
Harlequin® titles, free excerpts and more at
www.HarlequinInsideRomance.com.

REQUEST YOUR FREE BOOKS!
2 FREE NOVELS PLUS 2 FREE GIFTS!

◆ Harlequin®

ROMANTIC
SUSPENSE

Sparked by Danger, Fueled by Passion.

YES! Please send me 2 FREE Harlequin® Romantic Suspense novels and my 2 FREE gifts (gifts are worth about $10). After receiving them, if I don't wish to receive any more books, I can return the shipping statement marked "cancel." If I don't cancel, I will receive 4 brand-new novels every month and be billed just $4.24 per book in the U.S. or $4.99 per book in Canada. That's a saving of at least 15% off the cover price! It's quite a bargain! Shipping and handling is just 50¢ per book in the U.S. and 75¢ per book in Canada.* I understand that accepting the 2 free books and gifts places me under no obligation to buy anything. I can always return a shipment and cancel at any time. Even if I never buy another book, the two free books and gifts are mine to keep forever.

240/340 SDN FC95

Name _____ (PLEASE PRINT) _____

Address _____ Apt. # _____

City _____ State/Prov. _____ Zip/Postal Code _____

Signature (if under 18, a parent or guardian must sign)

Mail to the **Reader Service:**
IN U.S.A.: P.O. Box 1867, Buffalo, NY 14240-1867
IN CANADA: P.O. Box 609, Fort Erie, Ontario L2A 5X3

Not valid for current subscribers to Harlequin Romantic Suspense books.

Want to try two free books from another line?
Call 1-800-873-8635 or visit www.ReaderService.com.

* Terms and prices subject to change without notice. Prices do not include applicable taxes. Sales tax applicable in N.Y. Canadian residents will be charged applicable taxes. Offer not valid in Quebec. This offer is limited to one order per household. All orders subject to credit approval. Credit or debit balances in a customer's account(s) may be offset by any other outstanding balance owed by or to the customer. Please allow 4 to 6 weeks for delivery. Offer available while quantities last.

Your Privacy—The Reader Service is committed to protecting your privacy. Our Privacy Policy is available online at www.ReaderService.com or upon request from the Reader Service.

We make a portion of our mailing list available to reputable third parties that offer products we believe may interest you. If you prefer that we not exchange your name with third parties, or if you wish to clarify or modify your communication preferences, please visit us at www.ReaderService.com/consumerchoice or write to us at Reader Service Preference Service, P.O. Box 9062, Buffalo, NY 14269. Include your complete name and address.

HRS11

USA TODAY *bestselling author B.J. Daniels*
takes you on a trip to Whitehorse, Montana,
and the Chisholm Cattle Company.

RUSTLED

Available July 2011 from Harlequin Intrigue.

As the dust settled, Dawson got his first good look at the rustler. A pair of big Montana sky-blue eyes glared up at him from a face framed by blond curls.

A woman rustler?

"You have to let me go," she hollered as the roar of the stampeding cattle died off in the distance.

"So you can finish stealing my cattle? I don't think so." Dawson jerked the woman to her feet.

She reached for the gun strapped to her hip hidden under her long barn jacket.

He grabbed the weapon before she could, his eyes narrowing as he assessed her. "How many others are there?" he demanded, grabbing a fistful of her jacket. "I think you'd better start talking before I tear into you."

She tried to fight him off, but he was on to her tricks and pinned her to the ground. He was suddenly aware of the soft curves beneath the jean jacket she wore under her coat.

"You have to listen to me." She ground out the words from between her gritted teeth. "You have to let me go. If you don't they will come back for me and they will kill you. There are too many of them for you to fight off alone. You won't stand a chance and I don't want your blood on my hands."

"I'm touched by your concern for me. Especially after you just tried to pull a gun on me."

"I wasn't going to shoot you."

Dawson hauled her to her feet and walked her the rest of the way to his horse. Reaching into his saddlebag, he pulled out a length of rope.

"You can't tie me up."

He pulled her hands behind her back and began to tie her wrists together.

"If you let me go, I can keep them from coming back," she said. "You have my word." She let out an unladylike curse. "I'm just trying to save your sorry neck."

"And I'm just going after my cattle."

"Don't you mean your boss's cattle?"

"Those cattle are mine."

"*You're* a Chisholm?"

"Dawson Chisholm. And you are…?"

"Everyone calls me Jinx."

He chuckled. "I can see why."

*Bronco busting, falling in love…it's all in a day's work.
Look for the rest of their story in*

RUSTLED

*Available July 2011 from Harlequin Intrigue
wherever books are sold.*

Copyright © 2011 by Barbara Heinlein

HIEXP0711R

Looking for a great Western read?

We have just the thing!

A Cowboy for Every Mood

Visit

www.HarlequinInsideRomance.com

for a sneak peek and exciting exclusives
on your favorite cowboy heroes.

Pick up next month's cowboy books
by some of your favorite authors:

Vicki Lewis Thompson
Carla Cassidy
B.J. Daniels
Rachel Lee
Christine Rimmer
Donna Alward
Cheryl St.John

And many more…

Available wherever books are sold.

ACFEM0611R

From bestselling author

BEVERLY BARTON

Laying His Claim
(Silhouette Desire #1598)

After Kate and Trent Winston's daughter was kidnapped, their marriage collapsed from the trauma. Ten years later, Kate discovers that their daughter might still be alive. Amidst their intense search, Kate and Trent find something else they'd lost: hot, passionate sexual chemistry. Now, can they claim the happy ending they deserve?

**Ready to lay their lives on the line,
but unprepared for the power of love!**

Available August 2004 at your favorite retail outlet.

Visit Silhouette Books at www.eHarlequin.com   SDLHC

COMING NEXT MONTH

#1597 STEAMY SAVANNAH NIGHTS—Sheri WhiteFeather
Dynasties: The Danforths
Bodyguard Michael Whittaker was intensely drawn to illegitimate
Danforth daughter Lea Nguyen. He knew she was keeping secrets
and Michael's paid pursuit soon spilled into voluntary overtime. They
couldn't resist the Savannah heat that burned between them, yet could
they withstand the forces that were against them?

#1598 LAYING HIS CLAIM—Beverly Barton
The Protectors
After Kate and Trent Winston's daughter was kidnapped, their marriage
collapsed from the trauma. Ten years later, Kate discovered that their
daughter might still be alive. Amidst their intense search, Kate and Trent
found something else they'd lost: hot, passionate sexual chemistry. Now,
could they claim the happy ending they deserved?

#1599 BETWEEN DUTY AND DESIRE—Leanne Banks
Mantalk
A promise to a fallen comrade had brought marine corporal
Brock Armstrong to Callie Newton's home. He'd vowed to help the
widow move on with her life, but he'd had no idea Callie would call
to him so deeply, placing Brock in the tense position between duty and
desire.

#1600 PERSUADING THE PLAYBOY KING—Kristi Gold
The Royal Wager
Playboy prince Marcel Frederic DeLoria bet his Harvard buddies
that he'd still be unattached by their tenth reunion. But when he was
unexpectedly crowned, the sweet and sexy Kate Milner entered his
kingdom. Could Kate persuade this playboy king to lose his royal wager?

#1601 STONE COLD SURRENDER—Brenda Jackson
Madison Winters was never one for a quick fling, but when she met
sexy Stone Westmoreland, the bestselling author taught the proper
schoolteacher a lesson worth learning: when it came to passion, even
the most sensible soul could lose their sensibilities.

#1602 AWAKEN TO PLEASURE—Nalini Singh
Stunningly sexy Jackson Santorini couldn't wait to call a one-on-one
conference with his former secretary, Taylor Reid. But—despite his
tender touch—Taylor was tentative to enter into a romantic liaison.
Could Jackson seduce the bedroom-shy Taylor and successfully awaken
her to pleasure?

SDCNM0704